By The Short Hairs

short stories by

E.R. Wytrykus

"BY THE SHORT HAIRS"

Wheat Field Publications
109 Kiwi Court.
Lincoln, CA. 95648
NDWY2@aol.com

ISBN 978-0-6151-6434-2

INDEX

There's probably no such thing as reincarnation, and probably

no such thing as "Hell". But then again, how do we know? --erw

To Live And Die Again—And Again

After he died Joel Farthingale was confused. He knew he'd died because he'd attended the funeral, invisible, it seemed, to the handful of mourners. He'd also gone to his home, and he hadn't been in bed, so he was sure this wasn't a dream. But now, confronted by this creature, he wasn't sure of anything.

Except for his size and incredibly smooth features, there was nothing remarkable about the man behind the podium, other than his pair of wings. He stood about six and a half feet tall, with thick golden hair neatly trimmed to the tip of his ears. A flowered silk sport shirt covered shoulders and a torso that any body builder would appreciate. A large gold medallion hung loosely around his neck. It pictured a battle, with one creature cowering while above him a winged warrior raised his sword in triumph.

"Mr. Farthingale, how nice to see you. How are you?" The winged man smiled and Joel smiled back, weakly.

"I'm fine, I, I guess."

"For a dead man! Ha!" The winged man laughed at his joke, just as he'd done thousands of times before.

Farthingale's attempt at laughter caught in his throat. He asked, "Are you an angel?"

"Of course! But I see you don't remember me. How silly of me. After all these years I still can't get used to humans. I'm Rasiel. We've met in your other visits here."

"What other visits? When was I here? And where am I now?"

"Hold on, don't ask so many questions," Rasiel replied. "You've been here on several occasions, Mr. Farthingale, after each of your lives ended. Are you starting to remember?"

Blurry images flooded Farthingale's mind. He felt a headache coming on and closed his eyes. A feeling of déjà vu overwhelmed him. Slowly, reluctantly, a wall lifted and Joel's memory was loosened.

He saw the other car a split-second too late. Joel hadn't had much to drink, because he'd left the party early so he could meet his girl friend. But those few drinks were just enough to slow his reflexes, and by the time his foot found the brakes Joel had smashed his car into a parked truck, missing a pedestrian, but throwing himself through the front window. Unconscious already, his body landed with a crack on asphalt, then rolled and tumbled for thirty yards before coming to a stop, lifeless, against a fire hydrant.

Joel tried to shut off the scenes but they ran on, leading him through the funeral, the obligatory eulogy by his lying brother-in-law, and then he was driving a strange car along a strange road. The flat, unchanging desert landscape did seem vaguely familiar, but he couldn't recall ever taking a trip through the desert before; he'd lived his entire life in the comforting womb of concrete cities. For the first time he experienced that feeling of having been here before.

"It's a shame," he said aloud as he drove, "dying before I got that promotion. Damn, I worked hard for that! A couple more months and I'd have been in solid. And now this, when I'm only forty-seven. What rotten luck, just like always."

Farthingale always complained about his luck. But it hadn't been luck that he married his boss's daughter, nor that years later he got divorced and married the sister of his new boss. The fact that he'd loved neither woman Farthingale considered bad luck.

The car he was driving, a model he couldn't identify, was very comfortable. Oddly, there were no dials, no fuel gauge, no speedometer, no clock. Soothing music played, but he couldn't find the radio.

He wondered if anyone missed him. His foolish wife might, but she was the weak, crying type. His children and current mistress might miss him until after the reading of the will, when they wouldn't need to disguise their true feelings.

"Well, if this is death, I should be able to handle it. Already I've got a nice car and with my brains I should do all right wherever I end up." He hoped his ulcer, which often acted up in times of stress, didn't start bothering him. How can it if I'm dead, he thought.

The road led on endlessly, the car drove effortlessly, and for lack of anything to do Farthingale reminisced about his life. When he recalled the scant time he'd had for his family, the carousing in the name of business, the lies he'd told in the name of ambition, he wondered if he'd spend eternity driving forever, pondering a wasted life.

As dusk approached the desert came alive with exotic sounds of night creatures. The castle appeared suddenly, only a hundred yards away, shrouded in a shimmer of rising heat. A mirage, Farthingale thought.

The highway curved through an open gate, and the car slowed, but continued on into an empty, circular courtyard. Again Farthingale's memory tingled with the anticipation felt upon returning after a long absence to a place of poignancy.

Outside the car he shivered, and was surprised that the air had turned so cool so fast. He walked around the gray slab courtyard, his steps echoing solidly in the twilight. The yard was perfectly circular with walls punctuated at regular intervals by massive wood doors. Joel counted thirteen of the doors, an ominous number. Then he realized that the door through which he had entered had silently closed. He walked back to it and pulled and pushed, but it would not open. He tried all the doors but it wasn't until the last one, the thirteenth, that one opened.

A long hallway of red brick led towards a faint bluish glow. Farthingale prided himself on being able to adapt, advantageously, to changing conditions, but he didn't like being led; he was used to setting his own conditions. But now curiosity led him on.

The hallway ended in a round room bathed in a warm blue light. The floor was marble, white with streaks of gold. It melted into the bluish haze and met the walls in a cloud, then blended into an azure vapor that rose endlessly to an infinite ceiling. Three marble steps led to a platform, and at the top, behind a podium, stood what appeared to be a man, reading or writing; the haze made it difficult to see.

The blurriness evaporated, and Joel again saw the giant, Rasiel, and he shuddered and felt a twinge of fear, an alien emotion for him.

"I still don't understand. I saw myself—killed in a car crash—and I remember now how I got here, but what does it mean? What happens now? Am I dead or not?"

"Yes, you're dead, and no, you're not," said Rasiel, as he continued to leaf through a large book.

"You've been dead many times, and you've lived many times. Right now you're sort of in between."

"You mean I've lived other lives and been reincarnated?"

"Oh yes," answered Rasiel. "I'm not sure how many times but it's all here if you want to look at it."

"Rasiel handed Farthingale the gold book, about the size of a thick photograph album. Hundreds of photos filled the book, some with captions, some with dates.

"May 17, 1696; January 14, 1807; April 13, 1922, Farthingale read.

As he looked at the pictures they came to life, and Farthingale became fascinated with the movie. Only it was more than a movie because he was watching, and feeling, a person's life, and that person was himself, in different guises. He saw himself as a soldier huddling in a hole while battle raged all around.

"Sergeant, we've got to hit them from our side! They'll overrun the perimeter if we don't help! Sergeant Grogan!"

Shells rained down on the green troops trying to defend the thin line that separated the enemy from a rich cache of ammunition. Sergeant Grogan's platoon held a position on a small hill, just high enough to overlook the pastures through which the Germany army advanced. Meandering ditches streaked the land, scars of the Great War and the sluggish, ponderous killing that distinguished it.

"Sergeant, the Germans don't even know we're here. We could surprise them and give those other guys a breather."

Grogan looked coldly at the young soldier, and snapped, "Kid, I didn't survive this long by sticking my neck out. Let those idiots kill each other down there, and you can join them too, for all I care. But me, when it's dark, I'm getting out of here.

Grogan moved up onto his knees, faced the private and grabbed him by the collar. "And kid, one word of this by you or anyone else in this platoon and you'll find out that I can use this rifle if I have good enough cause to."

That night, with the battle bogged down to an occasional sniper shot that prevented rescue of the wounded, Grogan crawled out of his muddy sanctuary, quietly so as not to wake the others. He had scouted the area carefully, and studied the maps: to the south was a forested region that was still free of fighting. There he would abandon his uniform and changed into the simple workman's clothes he had stolen weeks earlier. The hell with this war!

"Not wanting to kill is a fine virtue, of course, but you abandoned your men and failed to assist your comrades." Rasiel was speaking and Farthingale looked up from the hypnotic pictures. His eyes were huge and glassy.

"This was me," he said, a statement, not a question. "And I was a coward".

"Worse!" cried Rasiel. "You betrayed a trust, deserted your responsibility. Now watch, Rasiel pointed to the book and Farthingale looked at it again. "And feel!"

Farthingale watched the movie in his book of life and death as he, Grogan, skulked away from his platoon. The sergeant was only yards away from the tree line when he heard a high-pitched whistle overhead. An errant shell, he knew immediately, and dashed for the woods. A white flash was the last thing Grogan saw, the thump as the shell hit the last thing he heard. Grogan felt nothing, dying instantly. In the blue room of the castle Farthingale convulsed in pain; his eyes burned from the brightness of the exploding shell, his chest and legs hurt as if someone had beat him with a club.

"Stop, stop, I'm dying!" he screamed.

"You can't die now, Mr. Farthingale," reminded Rasiel.

The pain stopped, his eyesight returned, and Farthingale breathed easier, though he was soaked with perspiration.

Rasiel pointed at the book, "Look some more, it's very interesting."

Like a masochist, knowing the book held pain but unable to resist it, Farthingale picked it up and looked again. A photograph showed several men sitting around a table, one of them Farthingale. As he watched, the picture came to life and the men were talking, arguing, smoking, laughing, and then attentive as Farthingale stood to give a presentation. Watching himself, Joel recalled the meeting, one of hundreds he'd attended, because of its significance in his career.

The photograph didn't stop there. It proceeded to follow Farthingale as he received congratulations on his research, his report, and his recommendations that would surely enhance the financial situation of the company. What startled Farthingale was the way the hidden camera followed him that evening as he kept a rendezvous with the executive of a rival company. Word for word, exactly as if he'd written the script himself, the photograph duplicated the exchange of marketing plans, the very plans Farthingale had just that afternoon outlined to his fellow executives and superiors.

Farthingale was not the least bit embarrassed that Rasiel had these events in his wondrous book, for he had considered them the highlights of his business career. Not only had several vice-presidents' heads rolled, but Farthingale, never under any suspicion of giving away his own ideas, was vaulted to a vice-presidency himself. The presidency of the company was not far away.

The photograph was still again; now it showed a grinning Farthingale vainly accepting congratulations on his promotion. The dead Farthingale looked up at Rasiel.

"Why couldn't you have let me live a little longer? I would've had the presidency soon, then I would have got that company moving. I would've made millions," he said, shaking his head sadly.

Rasiel smiled and fingered his gold medallion. "The company would have made millions before, if you hadn't sold your marketing strategy. You had your chance."

"I needed to work myself into a key position. In the long run it would have benefited," Joel explained.

"And in the short run your colleagues were accused of selling out, were fired, many of the factory workers were laid off due to loss of sales, including two workers whose marriages collapsed because of the financial problems that resulted."

"That certainly wasn't my fault," Joel protested. "Just because a couple people couldn't handle their own problems you can't blame me."

"I'm not here to blame you or to praise you or even to judge you, or to argue with you. I will try to point out some of the things you have done with your lives that have left us dissatisfied with your progress."

"Progress? Progress towards what? What am I supposed to be doing with my life?" Agitated now, Joel started to move towards the first step of the podium, but found that he couldn't get his legs started. He looked down, bent his knees, moved his arms, but his feet were frozen in place, as if locked in a block of ice.

"Don't get difficult, Bx 499. I don't want to have to discipline you the way I had to on your last visit."

"What did you call me?"

"That is your code name here. 'Farthingale' is simply the name you've used in your latest life.

"I can see that you need to learn more before we make new arrangements," the angel continued. "So I want you to turn to the brown pages in the book and look at the pictures there."

Farthingale did as he was told. A picture showed several people in a smoky room seated on large pillows. Their faces were blank; they might have died with their eyes open. Yet, as the picture became a movie that hypnotized

Farthingale the figures did move, slightly, dully. Glassy eyes and sluggish limbs staggered together in a slow-motion choreography.

Joel was perplexed. What did this have to do with him? He wasn't even in the picture.

"Of course you don't look the same," said Rasiel. "You're the chubby fellow with the dark skin."

Then Joel noticed the varieties of skin color and shapes in the people. There were green and black, blue and red skins. Very short people and very fat, some extremely tall and thin, some very beautiful; much like any heterogeneous group of people, except for the exaggerated dimensions. In the blue room Farthingale could feel his obesity, and felt languorous.

"Mkaalak, more Lysergy," someone called to the dark, fat man who Farthingale knew as himself. The man took something out of a small box and handed it to a green-skinned, yellow-haired woman, who in turn handed Mkaalak a plastic card. The woman broke open the item, a capsule, and poured the powdery contents into a glass of liquid, then drank the mixture down in one swallow. Almost immediately her eyes dilated, her mouth opened wide in a wicked grin, and she began to dance while humming to herself. Most of the others in the scene were doing the same by now.

"You make the best medicines, Mkaalak," a red man said to the fat distributor. "We'll be on high for weeks with this batch."

"A pleasant way to pass the time, friend," said Mkaalak, bowing slightly as a thank you.

"Hmmm, I remember vaguely," said Farthingale. It was a good business. I lived well from selling drugs. People didn't have much else to do with their time then, there, wherever this was; I can't remember that." He looked up at Rasiel for answers.

"Where it was doesn't matter. It was a different universe and a long time ago. It was the way you spent your life, a complete waste. You did not accomplish anything worth mentioning though you lived for over six hundred years."

"I just gave them what they wanted. What about them, what good did they do, if you say I wasted my life?"

"Never mind, that is not your concern. Every case is unique." Rasiel's deep voice lowered even more than usual, a note that frightened Farthingale.

"You've been given a good brain, not like others less fortunate. You've also been blessed with common sense, a quality that I wish had been distributed more liberally. So I won't need to spell out to you what you should do with your life or what you shouldn't do. That would make things too easy. Although I must admit it would make things easier for me, too," Rasiel added with an almost human tonality.

"Am I responsible for the habits of society? If society wants drugs and I can get it best, aren't I fulfilling a need, and doing what I do best?"

"Aha, this is what I like." Rasiel grinned in an eagerness for debate.

"Most people here are acquiescent, and I might add, penitent. But a good argument is interesting for a change. Obviously then, you've done some thinking about the moral responsibilities of a person."

"Well, I know I've always tried to be as successful as I could be. Nothing wrong with that, is there?"

"Basically, you're right, that's what people should do. But what about responsibility, commitment, trust, loyalty, love, and those ideals that humans put a lot of faith in?"

"You tell me," demanded Farthingale. "The least you can do is give me some advice."

"No, no, for all infinity! I can't make it too easy for you. You've seen your book, and every time you've seen people hurt because of your actions. Doesn't that tell you something about your values?"

"I didn't see anybody hurt by the drugs," Joel countered.

"That whole civilization stagnated. It died out before its time. The society had become so technically oriented that the people become blasé about doing things for themselves and neglected personal growth. They didn't even reproduce anymore. You died with them; you died of apathy."

"You talk about 'making arrangements' for me. It sounds like some sort of punishment," Joel said, his voice faltering, afraid that what he was thinking of would be his fate. "Am I going to hell?"

"I don't know," said Rasiel. "Do you think you deserve to?"

"No, why should I? I never killed anyone, never stole from anyone or went to jail. I may have fudged a little on my income tax, but everyone does that."

"Everybody does not," corrected Rasiel, "and if they did it wouldn't make it right."

"What about your wives?" the angel asked. "You've never been faithful to a one. Do you have an excuse for that?"

"Oh, I suppose I ran around a little when I was younger, but after I married I was almost faithful. Except for my secretary, but she was such a looker...!

"Well, then my secretary did have an abortion. I guess that was bad. Is that it, is that what I'll be punished for?"

Rasiel sighed, a deep, rumbling sigh that only a giant of a man, or an angel, could make, and he looked into another book he had in front of him, and said nothing for a few moments—moments that seemed like hours to Farthingale.

The man looked past the angel and around at the room. It was immense; rather, the smoky azure cloud hid the dimensions and gave the feeling of indefiniteness. Is this the entrance to Heaven? He'd been here for hours of human time, yet he didn't feel tired or hungry.

"Farthingale!" Rasiel's heavy voice called the man back to attention.

"No, that wasn't your worst sin. The soul of that baby was not lost. It was born again in another body. Your cheating on your wives, and cheating on your friends and business associates, were not your worst sins either, although highly reprehensible. Your dallying with every female you could lay your hands on in some of your younger days is understandable, though when you were Gavin Pendleton you did go a bit far."

"Gavin Pendelton? When was that?"

"That was in the twenty-fourth century, I believe, as you calculate time."

"The twenty-fourth! How can that be? It's only the twentieth century!"

"Oh, well, that doesn't matter. We live in all ages, all dimensions. Here, there are no days, hours, or years."

"But, as I was saying," Rasiel continued. "Your worst sin, if I could summarize all your lives, and especially your Farthingale years, was a lack of consideration for other people, combined with a lackadaisical attitude towards your responsibilities and commitments."

Rasiel gestured and Farthingale's eyes opened to the self-centered lives he had led. A rush of past lives flooded his memory, and sadness enveloped him like the steamy blue vapor that wrapped around his legs and curled upward, bringing an icy chill that startled him.

"I feel lonely," he sobbed.

"You've said that before. Almost every time you've been here you've said that. Yet you go back and live the same shallow life, over and over. What I've got to do now is to make a decision about your next destination. Somehow we've got to get you to use your good qualities so that you can end this wandering."

Farthingale slumped down into a chair he hadn't noticed before and looked up at the angel looming over him, the angel who held his destiny in his hands.

"Normally I just assign someone to wherever he's needed. But in your case, since we've had so little luck with you, I'm going to let you have a choice."

Suddenly aware, Farthingale stood up, adjusted his necktie, brushed his hair with his hands, and cleared his throat, as if priming himself for an important business meeting.

"What choices do I have? Can I go back to the same job?"

"No, we don't like to do that, though we can, and have. But it might be too hard for you to change the nature of Joel Farthingale. We prefer to send you somewhere new to start over. You can choose any century, any country, you can even be a female if you like."

Farthingale raised his eyebrows: If I could go back to early twentieth century, invest wisely, then when I'm Farthingale in the later twentieth century...his thoughts were shattered by Rasiel's booming voice.

"Forget it Bx 499! You forget where you are! Your thoughts might as well be written on your face. No, Farthingale, it isn't that easy, I keep telling you. One life doesn't remember the others under normal circumstances, though we do make exceptions. Euphorbus, Bridie Murphy, and so forth. Anyway, immortality isn't all that great, at least not as a human. Do you remember your life as a beggar in India?"

Dirt and lice were in his hair and under his fingernails and dull pains racked his body which cried out for nourishment. On the floor of the blue room Farthingale thrashed about, pulling his hair, shaking the lice off his arms, screaming and crying out wretchedly, and finally retching and choking.

"I can send you back to that Bx 499, and allow you to remember a life of pleasure you once lived! Where do you think Hell is, anyway?"

Rasiel stared down at Farthingale, who now lay exhausted on the floor. "Bx 499, you'd better shape up soon, for your own sake. From now on your lives will get harder, not easier. I don't want this to go on for longer than your universe exists, but here we have all the time there ever was, or ever will be, and we'll keep sending you back to live, again and again, and again—until you get it right!"

Baseball loves to keep its records and statistics. You want to know who led the National League in triples in 1913? You can look it up. Want to know how many times a certain player hit into double plays last season? You can look it up. But there are some things that don't show up in the record books, and they may be the most interesting stories. --erw

You Can't Look It Up

You can't look this up, because there aren't any categories for it in the record books. Every once in awhile some reporter will write a story about it, usually during those doldrum days just after the Super Bowl and before spring training has started. But their stories are never quite accurate. How could they be? None of them saw it as well as I did; in fact I don't think any of the reporters who were there that day--and there weren't many because it was a meaningless game between two floundering, beaten teams on a wet, dreary afternoon on the next to the last day of the season--are still writing today, if they're even alive. Some of the old ballplayers talk about it, too, but none of them saw everything the way I did, and you know ballplayers, they exaggerate like hell.

Like I said, it was a rainy, dreary afternoon, day before the season was supposed to end. Over in Chicago the Sox and the Yanks were playing and they were both battling for the pennant, so that's where most of the reporters were, except for a few locals. The Mavericks, dead last again, were meeting the Buckskins, just ahead of dead last again. Only the morbid cared which one of them won these last two games. It didn't matter because the two teams would end up with the worst records in the league for the fifth or sixth year in a row; I forget which.

But even mediocre, or I should say, lousy teams can put on an exciting ball game, if you like ball games. And this day they put on a game that couldn't be equaled for excitement, even if no one, except me, that is, really knew what happened.

Before I forget though, I should go back a few weeks to set the stage, so you'll have the whole picture. What happened was that Tiger Dan, you know, Tiger Dan Tanrahan, the Mavericks' best hitter-- although that's hardly saying anything with a team that had a combined batting average of .223-- but he was the best they had, and he could powder one a long way sometimes. In fact one day he hit one too far. Couple innings later he hit another monster, all the way out of the park, would you believe!

Well, Tiger Dan wasn't too smart, but he was ambitious, so he wanted to get three home runs in one game. When he came to bat in the sixth inning there was no doubt he was up there with only one purpose in mind. And the fans loved it, cheering for him long and loud. But a strange thing happened. Tiger Dan took a mighty swing, but didn't get a good piece of the ball—it rolled meekly out towards second base. The strange thing was that another ball rolled out towards shortstop! On top of that, Dan's bat had cracked and part of it flew towards third base. The third sacker jumped aside, but the rest of the infield was really busy.

The shortstop played his ball on a high hop, then stared at it as if he'd never seen a ball before. He looked up with his eyes wide open and his mouth agape. Meanwhile the second baseman had charged his ball and smartly scooped it up and thrown to first. Tiger Dan was thrown out, but he was already long gone, into the dugout. The umpire at home called timeout and walked out to the shortstop, who handed him, get this, a rubber ball!

To make a long story short, especially since this is just background, Dan's bat had broken apart and a rubber ball had popped out of a hollow part of the bat! Now I don't exactly know how this works, but somehow it is supposed to make the ball—-the one thrown by the pitcher, that is, go farther when the batter connects. I don't know if that's true, but I do know it's illegal, and sure enough, Dan was thrown out of the game. The other team protested that Dan's two homers should be disallowed, but the umpire said there is no proof that Dan had used the illegal bat when he hit those. Well, of course he did, you nitwit, how do you think he hit the blamed balls that far, and so on and on the argument went. But there wasn't anything the umpire could do about it.

Tiger Dan got himself suspended for several games. After that he was closely watched. Every time he got a hit the other team asked to check his bat to be sure it wasn't tampered with. Now, a good job of tampering can't be readily identified anyway, so I can't honestly say whether Dan continued to use an illegal bat or not. But as the batboy my job was to get the bats back into the dugout after the batter threw it down, but not to get in the way of the play on the field. So now I got new orders: whenever Tiger Dan batted my main concern was to get that bat quickly and hurry with it to the bat rack, before the other team could get their hands on it.

I know, I know, I guess I was a party to a crime. If I was told to get Dan's bat out of there then it must have been illegal, but what the heck, I was just a kid having the time of his life—I was batboy for a major league team, and how many kids did you know who could say that? So I did what I was told and kept my mouth shut.

So now we come to the day I mentioned, the one you can't look up anywhere because no one's ever written it correctly. The season was basically over for the Mavericks and the Buckskins; they were just fighting for the honor of avoiding last place, but I think I said that already. And I think I said it was dreary and rainy, but that needs repeating because it's so important. The field was so wet that normally the game would have been canceled, but the Mavericks couldn't afford a rainout now. The attendance had been low all season, except for the optimistic first month or so, and they weren't making much money. But this was Fan Appreciation Day, or some such thing, and there were free gifts and a big crowd, probably the biggest of the season except for that doubleheader against the Yankees when Whitey Olycyznak had dared the umpires, days ahead of time, to find out how he threw a spitter. They did find out, of course, you remember that story, which has been written up enough so I won't go into that now. Maybe later. But wow, what a brawl that was!

So it's raining. Not just a drizzle, but a good, steady rain. The home team decides whether or not to start the game, after that the umps are in charge. The Mavericks insisted the game start because the crowd was getting wet and annoyed, and the team needed to at least get five innings in to make it an official game and avoid having to refund the ticket money. The players grumbled but sloshed out onto field.

Tiger Dan batted in the first inning and sure enough, before the adoring home crowd, he cracked one a country mile. Everybody stood transfixed for a moment, watching the flight of the ball, trying to follow the tiny spot of white against the gray sky. Everybody but me. I did my job. I dashed out there and grabbed the bat and had it back in the rack before the catcher thought of it. He saw me as I picked it up and made a move, but I was already out of his reach. He gave me a scowl and shook his gloved hand at me.

The game went slowly because there were a lot of hits and a lot of errors and a lot of time spent kicking mud out of spikes and wiping off home plate. I don't remember what the score was, that you could look up. But I do remember several players slipping in the mud or on the slick grass. A couple of weak hitters, who really needed to help their batting averages, got hits when the outfielders just fell down and the ball went splashing by them. Then another player, Smokey Olson I think it was, fell flat on his face in the mud rounding first base trying for a double. The only reason he was safe was because the ball was so slippery that the outfielder couldn't get a grip on it and threw the ball into the stands, hitting the top of a fan's umbrella. Boy did he look funny standing there on second base with mud all over him. Smokey Olson, I mean, not the fan.

We must have been going a couple hours already when Tiger Dan came up again. He'd batted in the third inning, when the Mavericks scored a bundle, but he'd only popped up, so no one challenged the bat. Now in the fourth inning he came up with runner on first and second, no one out. I saw Dan pull his favorite bat out of the rack, a dark, scratched-up model that he seemed to hit especially well with. He'd rubbed it with mud while waiting in the on deck circle.

"Gonna' hit a homer, Dan?" I said, loving the rain and mud and the chance to be here getting my Maverick uniform all dirty. It was a joy to kneel down in the mud and not worry that Mom would be angry.

"I'll sure try, boy."

Dan stepped into the muddy mess that was the batter's box and moved clumps of wet earth around until he was comfortable. Then he lifted each foot in turn and knocked the mud out of his spikes with his black bat.

Now one thing I want to say now so you won't wonder about it later: this takes a little longer to tell than it took for the whole thing to happen. That's just the way it is in telling about an event that happens rather quickly. I mean, you know how long a play in baseball takes—the guy hits the ball, he runs to first, he runs to second, to third, then home, maybe there's a play, maybe a cut-off, and it's over in a few seconds. This play I'm going to tell you about took a little longer because of the weather, but not much more. Of course the argument lasted God knows how long; seemed they'd never quit arguing about it.

So to get on with it, Dan didn't swing until the fourth pitch. I remember that because he jabbered at the ump after a called strike, and the ump, Big Carl Jones, raised one finger of one hand and two fingers on the other, and made sure Dan saw them, just to show that that was the count, and no more talk.

Just when O'Doul released the next pitch the rain started to come down harder, much harder in fact, like someone had turned the faucet on full power. The sound of the bat hitting the ball was more of a 'splat' than a 'crack'. But Dan had it hit the ball very well, no doubt about that. Both the centerfielder and the right fielder turned their heads and started to run towards the wall. The runners on first and second took one quick look and were off; they could see the ball wasn't going to be caught. The catcher, Moose Moran, flipped off his mask and surveyed the situation: one runner coming in from second base, maybe another from first. He glanced over to where Dan had dropped his bat, looked at me, already rising to go after the suspect weapon, and made his decision. He calculated that the runner from second would score easily, but before the runner from first would get to home Moose could retrieve the bat and get back to his position guarding home plate. He turned towards the bat, which lay a few feet up the first base line. I was over near the dugout on the third base line, so I had longer to go. Had the positions been reversed I would have reached the bat with no trouble. But I was quick, and rather than go around in back of the umpire, as I was supposed to, I cut right across home plate. I remember looking up at the umpire as I did it and he gave me a disapproving look, to say the least.

Moose and I reached the bat at the same time. I got both hands on it while he got one, his other hand being encased in the huge catcher's mitt. But Moose was stronger than I was and he gave a lank and pulled the bat away from me, sending me sprawling backward into a patch of very damp mud. Moose ran back to home plate, holding the bat in one hand. Just then the runner from second base came soaring across the plate. His foot found a puddle and splashed mud and water into the umpire, who squawked like a frightened cat. Sitting in the mud, looking out towards the field, I had a good view of everything that was going on. Between first and second there were two base runners. Charlie Owens, who'd been on first, had slipped in the mud on his way to second. Tiger Dan came flying around first and almost ran over Charlie. Fortunately he saw his teammate in time and stopped before he passed him. So there was Dan helping Charlie get up out of the mud. Later accounts would sometimes say that Dan had passed Charlie, but that isn't so. Another account said one of the Buckskins players had tripped Charlie, but that's not true either, for none of them were near enough. The shortstop was stationed right at second base while the second baseman had run out into right-center field to receive the relay. But that's jumping ahead a bit.

You see, what had happened was that Flash Fetzler, in right field, had made a remarkable play. Somehow he'd managed to catch up with the ball that Tiger Dan had stroked, probably because the damp air held it up for a second or so longer than normal. Flash dove for the ball and just got the tip of his glove on it; had he caught it cleanly it surely would have been a triple play. Flash went sliding head first on the soaked grass for several feet—his uniform acquired a long green stripe! Then the centerfielder, whose name I can't recall, got there and stumbled over Flash's sliding body. He fell face down and knocked himself out, while the ball rolled to a stop a few feet away. Boots Jensen, the second baseman, had moved out for the relay, as I said. Now he was hustling after the ball, which he got to before either of the outfielders could recover. Right on top of things the second base umpire had hustled out to see if the ball would be caught. Unfortunately he was right in line with Boots, who picked up the ball, turned, and fired it towards second base without even looking. The ball hadn't traveled more than twenty-five feet when it hit the man in blue square in the forehead! The umpire went down like he'd been shot—I think he thought he'd been shot! Believe it or not—I really don't care if you believe it—the ball bounced back to Boots, who caught it and threw it again to the shortstop. By this time Charlie and Tiger Dan were up on their feet, after sloshing around a bit, and were charging towards third base.

Moose was waiting at home plate, glove on one hand, bat in the other. I heard the ump yell at him to put the bat down. Moose could see now that both runners would get to home at about the same time, and that the ball would finally be coming in too. He had a moment of indecision as he looked from the field to the bat, and back to the field. He did a strange thing then: he stuck the bat behind him, in his belt! Most of it was sticking out, waving around as he moved. But Moose wasn't going to let go of that bat—he was sure Dan had used an illegal bat again and he was going to prove it, once things had calmed down around home plate.

So there it was: two runners screaming down the third base line, the ball in the shortstop's hands as he turned to throw to home, the umpire in back of Moose wiping mud out of his eyes, Moose standing like the Colossus of Rhodes, and me, sitting in the mud a few feet up the first base line. I had the best seat in the house.

If Charlie and Tiger Dan could have been running at full speed, unhindered by mud, the combined force of their bodies probably would have knocked even a huge man like Moose Moran into the third or fourth row of the box seats. But Charlie slipped again just he was starting to slide, and instead of sliding he stumbled into Moose, with Tiger Dan crashing into Charlie from behind. Moose caught the throw from the shortstop at the exact moment that Charlie smashed into him.

Have you ever heard an anvil being dropped onto a wet lawn from a height of about forty feet? Well, I haven't either, but that's what the collision sounded like. Charlie and Moose seemed to be suspended in time, neither force willing to give in. A split second later Tiger Dan joined the collision in process, every bit comparable, I thought, years later while reading an astronomy book, to the billion-years long collisions of galaxies, which through a telescope seem to be happening in slow motion, but in reality are happening at speeds impossible to comprehend.

This added jolt moved things along. Specifically, it moved Charlie and Moose, as one object, up into the air and over home plate, knocking the umpire flat on his back. Not only that, but remember the bat, dangling out of the back of Moose's pants? Naturally it couldn't stay there; too much was going on to expect an inanimate object to calmly stay put in such a precarious position, especially with such an enticing target as Big Carl's bald head, shining brightly with all the water on it! Sure enough the bat popped out of Moose's pants when he got hit by Charlie and cracked Big Carl on the top of that beautiful bald head, the coup de grace for him.

The ever-so-momentary resistance of the bodies of Charlie and Moose kept Tiger Dan from barreling on through, and he bounced back up the base line. The ball, the usually white spheroid now tainted by grass stains and mud blotches, squirted out of Moose's glove and spun in the mud, digging a tiny track in the mud right into my lap!

No one saw that, not even me. All eyes were on the conglomeration of bodies at home plate. A second later I would look down and see it sitting there, as if it were recovering from the violence going on around it.

For what seemed like a long time, but probably wasn't, no one moved. The umpire, Moose, Charlie, Tiger Dan, they were all down and out, at least momentarily dazed. The first base umpire rushed over to call the play. But when he looked in Moose's glove there was no ball. But neither Charlie nor Tiger Dan were on home plate so he had no idea whether they had tagged home.

Players from both teams dashed out of the dugouts. A couple of the Maverick players tried to revive their base runners and urge them to the plate, while the Buckskins looked for the ball and hollered that the Mavericks shouldn't be helping prone base runners.

The first and third base umpires, the only two that were conscious, tried their best to maintain control. Still, no call had been made. The rain was coming down in buckets now and most of the fans had retreated to the dry areas of the stands. On the field another crowd was growing, as every player on both teams shoved his way into the bunch huddled around home plate.

Finally one of the Buckskins players, after almost stepping on me, looked down and saw me holding the ball. A giant, he reached down and tore it from my grasp.

"Here it is, I've got it!" he screamed, then ran over and tagged first Charlie and then Tiger Dan. The latter, though, was on his feet already and standing on home plate, with the assistance of a couple of teammates. The Mavericks were shouting, "Safe! He's safe!"

I said only I could tell the story accurately, but even I can't remember all the things that were said, screamed, and cursed in those next moments. At my tender age I didn't understand a lot of the words, anyway. But you can fill that part in; it was the usual hysterical bellowing that goes on when men playing a kid's game don't get their way. Pretty soon the noise of the rainstorm and thunder drowned out (no pun intended) the noise of the shouting ballplayers—and two umpires—and the argument began to die down. Everyone wanted to get out of the storm now. There still hadn't been a "Safe!" or "Out!" call but I did hear one of the surviving umpires say that they'd decide about it in the locker rooms.

It was a good thing someone remembered about the umpire in the outfield, the one who'd been knocked out by Boots' throw, otherwise he might have lain out there all night and drowned! But after all the bodies had been dragged off the field and everybody, by now soaked to the bones, had had a chance to sit still for a moment the belligerency died down. Then someone laughed. Both teams had gone into one locker room, ostensibly to continue the discussion about the play, but once there someone laughed, then another person laughed and soon everybody was howling, roaring with laughter.

"That's the craziest play I've ever seen!"

"Did you see Boots conk ole Stinky Smithers? Now that's what I call an error, Boots!"

"Error! Hell, it's one of the best throws he's ever made!"

"Did you see those guys sliding around in the mud? They were funnier than Laurel and Hardy!"

"I don't know what the rule is. I don't think you're allowed to help them up."

"Yeah, they should be out, we tagged them!"

"Yeah!"

"Oh, yeah? Where'd you get the ball? How do we know that was the right ball?"

"Who cares? It was a ball, wasn't it?"

The players settled down to drying off, then they started eating, had a beer or two, and forgot about the game. Here were two teams in the basement of the league, and whether they won or lost or got rained out wasn't going to change the world. A couple hours later, when the flood warnings were issued by the weather bureau, the game was called off. As it'd only gotten into the fourth inning it wasn't an official game. No call had yet been made on the play at the plate, and now it didn't matter. Shrewdly the umpires decided to answer all queries with, "No comment," or "It's irrelevant, boys, so let's not worry about it."

It continued to rain the next day, too, so that game was rained out and that was the end of the season.

Tiger Dan's bat? Well, I did get one souvenir out of this, and hanging in my garage, along with a few other mementoes I gathered during my batboy career, is a long black, scratched-up piece of wood, with ragged tape around the handle. Was it hollowed out and filled with rubber balls? I don't know, I never checked.

This story is from those great days working at Parkview Supermarket, a job that started when I was only 15 and carried through high school and college. And I swear this is a true story. -- erw

Old Nick

Old Nick had a dead arm. Nothing lived in his right arm, no blood, and no nerves. He had no feeling in it, and there wasn't much it was good for. To set it anywhere he had to lift it with his left arm. The hand, of course, was no good either. He couldn't even hold a cigarette, and he always wanted a cigarette.

I can't remember how his arm was injured. To hear him tell it he had been a hero in the war, having saved several lives before being shot in the arm. He had the scars on the arm to prove it, and somewhere, if he could find it, he had a Purple Heart. Some day he'd bring it to the store and show us.

But somebody else, I think it was his sister-in-law, said that one winter night he had passed out, again, in an alley back of a tavern, and almost froze to death. Somehow he survived but his right arm had died.

"I wish all of him had died," she said many times. "He's a curse on the family."

Maybe he was, but how could a guy who gave us so many laughs be that bad?

Back then when things didn't have to be so much by the book, the store gave Nick a job. He wasn't on the payroll, which you couldn't do now, but he was paid some cash each week and allowed to eat whatever he could scrounge up. Across the street was a bar that also gave him odds jobs to do and provided him with a room, separated from and locked out from the bar itself, where he could sleep.

He spent most of the day at the store, sometimes from eight in the morning until eleven at night. A good thing for him, for otherwise he'd be out drinking or trying to find a drink and getting in trouble somewhere. We kept him in the backroom...like a crazy relative he wasn't allowed in the store among the customers. With his permanently reddened eyes and toothless grin we didn't want him to scare anybody. He looked old, but I was young so what did I know about old? He could have been thirty-five or he could have been sixty. No one knew and when asked, Nick wouldn't tell.

Nick had learned to handle a broom with his one good arm, and he could discard trash, break down cardboard and sort and stack the returned empty bottles. And he had stories galore, though no one believed any of them.

Eventually we even let him check in the bread deliveries. Checking in the bread was an important function, so Nick only handled the afternoon deliveries. In the morning the deliveries included coffee cakes and other sweets so it was important to 'contract' with the bread man what the charge would be today for his shelf space. Once the bread man was gone, there was little to stop us from hiding his bread behind other brands, that is, if we hadn't had an adequate breakfast!

Some people were downright mean to Nick. It was cruel, and the worst offender was his sister-in-law; she worked at the store, so she set the tone. But most of us treated him like one of the guys and included him in the jokes and the bullshit sessions. He was fun to play a trick on though, because he would always fall for it and then feign a terrible anger, though we knew he was actually glad to be included in the fun.

In the alley back of the store was a caged-in area connected to the wall of the store where we stored the returned empty bottles, and where Nick spent much of his time sorting the bottles. Other than a naked bulb with a pull-string there was no other light and it got awfully dark on a winter's night once the sun set. So usually the light was just left on all the time.

It's not unusual to catch mice in a grocery store. We had traps set up all the time. Who thought of this I don't know but somehow, someone, managed to tie a dead mouse by the tail to the pull-string of the bottle cage light bulb. And then we shut off the light.

We knew Nick would bitch and moan about the light because there was no way to turn it on except to go out in the cage and pull the string. And it was absolute, pitch dark.

"Goddamn it you guys, mumble, sonofabitch, blah, blah, mumble. Now I got to stumble through the dark why do you guys do this?"

The poor guy. We're lucky he didn't have a heart attack right there and then when his hand pulled that string. Yuck! The thought of it still gives me shivers. I don't think I ever heard, before or since, including my time in the army, such a string of profanities. Nor do I remember a better reason for such language.

But back to Nick's arm. It could do amazing things. Yes, I remember, I said it was useless and couldn't do anything. Not by itself, anyway.

Brazil nuts: big, chocolate colored, with an extremely hard shell. We had another name for them but it isn't nice to repeat. A nutcracker and persistence might crack one open but a hammer was better.

The floor of the back room of the grocery store was basic concrete. Hard, cold, basic concrete. Now take your arm and swing it down against the floor as hard as you can. It might not kill your arm but I'll bet for a few days it'd be as useless as Nick's. Now take some of these Brazil nuts and scatter them on the floor. Now bet a salesman that we have a guy here who can break these nuts with his bare hands. Impossible, they'd all say.

Nick would kneel on the cold floor over the Brazil nuts. He'd hold his right arm in his good left arm and then wind up, sort of like a pitcher getting ready to unleash his best fastball. He'd slap his dead arm down on the Brazil nuts as hard as he could! It hurt us to see it, to hear the smack of dead flesh against concrete. The nuts scattered everywhere, splattered into pieces almost too small to eat. Never seen anything like that!

I don't know what became of Nick. Eventually the work rules changed; you couldn't have someone 'off the books' working in the backroom. I think he still had a job cleaning up at the bar across the street, and he had done a pretty good job of staying sober, since that was one of the requirements of allowing him to work at the market. I got drafted soon after college, and never did see him again, nor do I remember hearing what happened to him. I'd like to think that he stayed sober and happy, cleaning up at the bar, and that when he passed on and someone looked through the meager belongings in his tiny room, they found a Purple Heart.

A vignette from my days in Vietnam; this is also an excerpt from my novel, 'The Money Run.'--erw

At The Berm

Bien Hoa airbase, a stone's throw from the finance unit I was assigned to, was the busiest airport in the world round about 1968 and 1969. Mostly that was due to jet fighter activity, but it also was the welcoming base for thousands of troops coming into Vietnam for their tour of duty. They came with lots of cash, none of it legally useful. Among the duties my unit had was to exchange Army script for this cash, prepare the paper work to account for it, pack it up in wooden footlockers, and truck it to Saigon, from where it was, I suppose, repacked and shipped back to the States. A run would consist of several footlockers loaded with three or four million dollars and three scared-shitless finance clerks to guard it against an enemy attack. In reality the route from Bien Hoa to Saigon was a well-traveled and well-protected busy highway, Route One, and the two runs I'd made already had been uneventful. I expected this one to be no problem and for it I would get a day off.

I had come through here myself recently. Some things the military does with such precision and so well organized that one can only stand back in awe. Then there are other things they do that make one ask, 'Is anyone in charge here?'

That's what it was like when I and a couple hundred other newbies climbed down after a flight that stopped in Hawaii, tempting us to stay in the hotel bar rather than return to the plane once it was refueled, in Guam, and again at Clark Field in the Philippines.

You'd think there'd be someone to tell us where to go and how to get there. Maybe a sign spelling out 'Da Nang', or 'Saigon', or '10th Finance'. But it was two hundred guys bumping into each other trying to figure out where to go. As it turned out I was in rock-throwing distance from my destination; I just didn't know it yet. Finally I bumped into a guy who had a jeep and was looking for lost souls like me. He took me to my new base, a quick five minute ride that kicked up enough dust for a brigade of tanks.

10th Finance was a rinky-dink looking collage of huts and wooden walkways connecting the various buildings. The wooden planks that made up the walkways would come in handy during the rainy season. It was September when I arrived and near the end of the dry season. The ground was a dusty yellow and gray composite, but the sky was a beautiful blue; too beautiful, it seemed, for a place of such chaos and death.

My driver guided me to a Sergeant named Eddie Graham who said he was expecting me and welcomed me like a long lost son. He showed me the desk where I would be working and told me to take the day to get oriented and he'd see me tomorrow. I was shown where I would live then directed to supply. There I was issued a blanket and pillow, a mattress thinner than a pancake, a rifle, flak jacket and helmet. The latter three items I could have done without. I mean, this is a finance company, isn't it? What the hell do I need a rifle and helmet for?

The next day, before I could report to Sgt. Graham, I was informed I first had to practice at the firing range. First with my rifle, then a machine gun, then a grenade launcher. I did okay; in basic training I actually had been one of the best sharpshooters, a feat I feared might send me to the infantry.

The company had a captain, but I think I only saw him once. It was a Lieutenant who ran things. I saw him almost every day, and sometimes he was sober. There was a Master Sergeant who thought he was the Army's answer to Captain Queeg and had us out on Sundays building up the berm that surrounded the base. Fortunately he left shortly after I arrived and things settled down to a nice, easy pace.

This morning I was stone tired, having been awake nearly the entire night on guard duty at the berm. It had been raining for several days and the ditches surrounding our camp were head-deep in water. To get to the perimeter bunkers we'd had to wade through the ditches. So at five o'clock yesterday afternoon I was soaked to the skin, and I stayed that way until eight this morning. Usually two of the three guards would stay awake while one caught some sleep. But as wet as we were it had made sleep impossible. Fortunately in the morning I'd had time to change to dry clothes and grab a quick breakfast, and, thanks be, it had stopped raining.

My previous plan for the morning had been to sleep three or four hours then dash over to the above ground pool the engineers had dug out for the local units. Mostly it was for the use of the grunts coming in from the field. Here they could relax in the sun, take a dip in clean water, and try not to think about going back into the fire zones for a few days. For those of us lucky enough to be stationed in the vicinity it was an unexpected luxury. Occasionally as I sat there soaking up the rays and reading a book or dozing, helicopters would whirl overhead. They carried soldiers, wounded ones, laid out on stretchers attached to the 'copter. Some of the poor slobs likely expired before medics or a mobile hospital could be reached. The sight caused a tinge of guilt to seep in and usually I'd stay away from the pool for a week or so until I'd forgotten about it. It wasn't until years later, when the television show M*A*S*H was popular that I recalled the scenes, almost exactly like the opening segment of the show.

Our driver was the guy called Tater, from Idaho. He was a Sergeant again, having been busted down and promoted up more times than even he remembered. With a military driver's license and contacts in the motor pool he was constantly going places he wasn't supposed to, when he wasn't supposed to. And sometimes he got caught. But he knew the streets of Saigon like a native taxi driver so when some visiting officer needed transportation likely as not Tater got a stripe back and the job of ferrying the brass around. Having an experienced driver was some compensation for having to sit in back with Bill Joyce.

Joyce was quirky. He spent all his free time doing his laundry and polishing his boots. He starched his fatigues until they could stand at attention and polished his boots until they shone like the morning sun twinkling off the still waters of Crater Lake. Many a night I awoke to see him using his cigarette lighter to inspect his boots and melt the polish into the leather.

"Kerist, Joyce, go to sleep already," someone would yell.

In the morning Joyce would awake with smoker's cough, reach under his bunk for the first of his two dozen a day cans of Coca-Cola, take a swig of the warm liquid, cough some more, and light his first cigarette of the day. Still, to talk to him he seemed like a normal, sane person. He was just a fanatic about his clothes and addicted to nicotine and caffeine. To tell the truth, I didn't know what he might be like in a stressful situation—a combat situation, but because of his weird habits it was assumed he wouldn't be much help. But then, I didn't know what I would do either.

We were finance people, our unit was the 10th Finance Company and if I never had to handle a rifle or duck for cover it was okay with me. But the first day there I was given my rifle, my flak jacket, helmet, and other gear, *just in case*, I was told. Also, I soon found out, we were expected to handle the perimeter guard duty at night and assist in case of enemy attack at any time.

Being in the shadow of the air base and of a brigade of the 101st Airborne put us in the line of fire for the frequent Viet Cong artillery and mortar attacks. Our main concern was for short rounds, those that didn't quite make it to the target. And, if the VC did break through our perimeter they could theoretically sneak around and attack the air base and its valuable jets from point blank range. A turn on this all-night duty came around about once every five nights, and actually lasted from five in the afternoon until eight in the morning. There were always three of us to a bunker so you could get some sleep, depending on the noise level. We were well armed with an M-80 machine gun pointed out our bunker across the field and with boxes of ammo and grenades, plus our own rifles. Wire fences and a minefield made it unlikely anyone would get through, but better safe than sorry.

Commercial jets bringing in new blood often landed at night, coming in over the field that sprawled between 10th Finance, the air base, and the village of Bien Hoa. To make it difficult for those nasty mortars to spot them the planes kept their landing lights off until the last possible moment. In our bunkers we could hear them (I think they were stretched 737s) as they came in for a landing. But we could not see the planes until they suddenly turned on their lights, just about the time they swept over our bunkers. They soared in so low over us I know absolutely I could have hit those planes with a rock if I tried. Between those planes and the roaring F4 Phantom fighter jets it was too noisy to talk to your buddy until very late, and then it could be deathly quiet until near dawn, when the jets awoke and screeched off on their way to early morning action.

There was a string of about a dozen bunkers around our camp. Most of the action was when monkeys or pigs scurried around in the field. The initial noise always gave us a stop---was there anyone out there? Eventually a grunt or a screech would identify the intruder. Worse, and scarier, was when one of the animals got close to the fence and set off a mine. If one of us did hear or see (or think we heard or saw) something out there we were to call it in to the Tower guards and request flares to light up the field. (We had enough ammo to start a new war but we weren't trusted with flares). One night one of the guys a couple bunkers down from mine was sure there were enemy soldiers crawling through the field coming right at him. Those of us in the other bunkers listened in on our radios to his conversation with the Tower. His request for flares became more frantic. The Tower was reluctant, probably because they knew a plane full of 'newbies' was due in and they didn't want too much light on the area.

"Are you sure, Bunker 5? You know there are pigs out there."

"This ain't no pig, Tower. I can see something, about a hundred yards out."

"Bunker 5, I doubt you can see a hundred yards out in the dark."

"Well, then they're even closer! Give me some light!"

"Negative. Give us a chance to survey the area."

This went on for several minutes while the rest of us strained our eyes to see if we could spot any movement in the darkness. Finally, the Tower came back on.

"Okay, Five, we will set off a flare over your area."

"Oh, man, we're all dead already!"

Well, it was nothing. In fact, the only time we ever had any excitement was when I heard movement outside our bunker, in *back* of us. Rifle in hand I cautiously looked out and spoke the password. I think it was 'Good' and the proper response was supposed to be 'Ugly'. I didn't get any reply except a groan and a cough. I saw something move and called out, "Drop your rifle!" My two partners were alerted by then and we all aimed at a shape that we could just barely see in the dark, a shape that seemed to tumble over as we approached it. Fortunately the intruder meekly lay down his gun. Then he puked. It was one of ours; some guy high as a kite and stumbling his way towards the minefield. Turns out he was a short-timer; only a couple days from freedom and he'd begun celebrating with booze and pot. We called the MPs and our prisoner was taken away to sober up.

But many more times than the one day in five of bunker duty were the times we were rousted from our cots in the middle of the night to hunker down in the crude shelters within our base camp area. This happened whenever there was enemy artillery or mortar action. Often we spent the rest of the night in these trenches, not much more than sandbags piled up with a metal roof and wooden benches lining the inside. We'd try to sleep sitting up while we waited for the all-clear signal. After a few weeks a soldier could tell the difference between the outgoing shells of the artillery unit that guarded the air base and incoming rounds fired by the Viet Cong. Those of us who had learned this would be out of bed and grabbing our boots and helmets even before the warning siren went off. By morning we would be both tired and high; there were always a few who decided this was a good time and place to suck those reefers. In the confined quarters the sweet scent reached all of us. So all in all, we were tired most mornings whether we were on guard duty or spent the night in a bunker or in our bed in the hooch. If it wasn't roaring jets it was thunderous rain. If it wasn't rain it was the thump of mortars. Most days our hour and a half of lunch break consisted of a quick bite and then a nap.

Right after we finished our regular workday, for those who didn't have to head to the bunkers for the rest of the day and night, there was basketball and volleyball. Jungle volleyball, we called it, because there were very few rules to consider. None of this pansy stuff like you couldn't touch the opponent while blocking his shot. We would play until about a half hour before the mess hall closed, then dash over for dinner. If it was still light after we ate we might play some more. At night there were often first-run movies, although if there was any sign of potential enemy activity nearby we couldn't have movies because the lighted outdoor screen was too big a target.

So it's March, 1969 in Vietnam. I've been here seven months already and spent Christmas playing volleyball and enjoying a steak we'd bar-b-que using an ammo carrier as a grill. But we did get to see the Bob Hope show with Ann-Margret last week, and then snuck over to the USO for a dinner slightly better than we got in our own mess hall. Because of the less than brilliant talents of our cooks a bunch of us would get together on weekends and purchase steak from the mess hall and cook them ourselves. Somebody, Tater probably, obtained charcoal and that and a few cheap beers made for relatively pleasant Sunday afternoons. The poor steaks would otherwise have been either burned to a crisp in the mess hall or ended up in the officer's mess.

But today it's the money run, and I'm sitting on top of more money than I knew existed, and probably more money than I'll ever be close to in the real world as long as I live. The back flap of the truck is open so as we barrel down the highway we can look back and see what we've passed. Small farms and hovels, oxen, people working in rice paddies and kids playing in the dirt or chasing chickens, the road busy with natives on bicycles and Americans in jeeps and trucks. I start to get sleepy and began to doze off even as we bounce along, sitting on our fortune.

Normally the run is smooth and uneventful. Once we deliver the strongboxes of dough we hit the USO for a beer or two, maybe catch some dinner at a local restaurant. The food is palatable; chicken, I think, I hope not dog; and vegetables and rice. At least here it doesn't smell as awful as the lunch of the kids and women who work around our compound. The smell of fish heads and rice cooked in some kind of gluey fish oil is enough to make one swear off seafood.

And again, normally, we have an officer with us on the run. Lieutenant Walsh was in a jeep and planned to meet us in Saigon. On the previous runs I participated in he rode up front, and after we were finished with business would treat us to the first beer. It depended on the time; we needed to leave early enough to get back to Bien Hoa before dark. Traveling along the highway after dark was even money for an ambush.

On my first run, which I thought would be my last, we left very early, had time for drinks and a meal, and climbed into the truck for the return trip. Tater was the driver then, too, and even with a few beers in him we felt confident he could find his way back home. Just head down Highway One. But the damn truck wouldn't start. I'm not mechanically inclined, so I was no help then and even years later I can't remember what the problem was. Generator, alternator, who knows. Tater knew who to contact but it was too late in the day to get the part and make the repair. So we had to find a place to hunker down for the night.

This night was the only night of my life that I slept with a rifle by my side. It's easy to say, yeah, a night on the town in Saigon, with all them pretty oriental ladies eager to please. But we'd heard too many stories of GIs who simply disappeared, were mugged or drugged, or, maybe worse, contracted some sort of disease that nothing, not penicillin or anything in our medicine cabinets could combat, and who were listed as missing in action and kept as virtual prisoners on some remote island in the Pacific. Now for the most part we didn't believe those stories, but as it got later and darker the noise of the drunks, the occasional gunshots and screams made us clutch our rifles in an almost paranoid bonding in our musty hotel room. More than once someone would pound on the door, 'Hey, GI, number ten mamasan! Good nookie! Only two dollah!' And we would yell back , 'Diddy Mao!, or other equivalents of 'Get the hell out of here!' in English, French and Vietnamese, fearful that at any second a grenade would come crashing through the window. It's not that any of us feared getting laid, we just feared getting dead.

But we survived, with little sleep that night. We got the truck fixed in the morning and laughed about our adventure all the way back to Bien Hoa. These were the adventures I never wrote home about; didn't want to worry Mom.

Since I like science fiction, I thought I should write a sci-fi story. So here is my little, cynical contribution to the genre. By the way...this is an old story from my files...I actually wrote it in 1981.-- erw

The Final Search

"But it isn't fair!" cried Akron. "You deserve the honor more than anyone". Had no sound come from his lips the arm-waving and fidgety posture would have shown the irritation in the young man.

"No one ever guaranteed that life would be fair," replied Horatio.

Akron leaned forward, started to say something, then stood up and walked to the only window in the room, the office of his uncle, Horatio, Mathematics and Computer Programming Dean of the World Science College. He turned toward his uncle, who sat at his desk, feet up, arms in back of his head, content to enjoy his pipe and determined not to let his nephew's tirade interfere with the treasured peacefulness of his private office.

"Don't you care that they awarded the chancellorship to that...that chemistry witch-doctor? It was you who developed the Capek-100, which is, I believe, the first technological breakthrough in computers in centuries."

"Don't be sarcastic," Horatio softly admonished. "I know quite well what it is we have developed."

"We? You developed it, Uncle Horatio. I just helped a little, you know that." Akron turned away and stared blankly out the window at the bustling campus.

"Your pretense at modesty doesn't fool me. You were a great help to me, Akron, and you want me to be named chancellor so our family name will be honored, which just might make you famous too. Maybe you even expect to be named to succeed me as Math and Computer Dean?"

Akron pivoted suddenly to face his uncle, his mouth agape and eyes wide. Horatio did not turn to meet his nephew's quizzical look, for he was too occupied with packing double-vanilla tobacco into his pipe. But as if on cue he said, "Don't give me that innocent, 'who, me?' look of yours, Akron. I know you too well."

Now Horatio did look at Akron. He pointed with his pipe, which Akron knew meant a serious comment was coming.

"You've always been concerned with honors and glory. That's fine in school, when it's practical to try to do your best. But glory for its own sake doesn't matter in the long run. We all die and when we do what does it matter if somebody names a building after us, or a spaceship, or even an entire planet? All that matters is the kind of life we lived. Now don't interrupt me...sit down and listen to what I have to say."

Akron did as he was told. Obstinate, effusive, sometimes clever to the point that acquaintances didn't trust him, Akron did respect his uncle, both because Horatio deserved respect for his accomplishments as a scientist and because Akron knew it was to his advantage to stay on good terms with someone of the stature of Prof. Horatio.

Horatio continued. "You've been bitter ever since your father returned from the war and did not receive the high honors he deserved. I agree, his success in ending the conflict was magnificent, but his knowing that was honor enough for him."

"He should have been named Military Chief," said Akron.

"He really didn't want that. He was ready to retire. Running around the galaxy had worn him out. Do you think he ended the Galactic conflict by blasting space cruisers to smithereens? No, he ended it with diplomacy, something few people understood. When he returned he was mentally exhausted and the citizenry were so eager to get on with colonization and mining that they didn't care who had ended the conflict, or how. They were tired of hearing about it and having theirs lives restricted by it."

Horatio puffed deeply on his pipe, remembering his brother.

"Had he been a great warrior a thousand years ago they would have built statues for him, though to what purpose I really don't know."

"He still deserved better than to be forgotten."

"Forgotten? By whom? I remember him; you remember him. His many friends remember him with great fondness. The people who knew him remember your father as a kind, loving person, not as a famous warrior. The memories he left us are all the glory his name needs. You'd do well to remember that, young man."

Horatio puffed the sweet fragrance from his pipe into a tiny cloud around his head. A busy, hardworking man, he found relaxation in two ways—his favorite pipe, a gift from his brother who'd had it hand-made on a far-away planet from the sweetest wood this side of the Andromeda Galaxy, and an occasional glass of single malt Scotch, especially from the Scotland district of planet Earth. Both pastimes he'd promised to indulge in more after his retirement, of which he now spoke to Akron.

"Akron, the Dean of Mathematics and Computers is not a prestigious position to the public. But it is to one's colleagues because they realize the importance of math to all sciences. But the job requires more than a knowledge of math. It requires understanding and concern for your colleagues. With all the great discoveries that science has made it is still people who decide what must be done, it is people who program our robots and computers, and it is people who we live with. Honors are nothing these days because technology has made what used to be startling discoveries commonplace. Communication is instantaneous. Nothing surprises people anymore."

"What are you getting at, uncle?" The question was put politely but the young man's impatience was starting to show.

Horatio came as close to a sigh as his calm manner would allow. "What I'm getting at is that I have one more job I want to do before I give up my position here. It is something I want to do more than to be dean of the entire university. And I want you to help me with this project."

"Does it have something to do with the Capek-100?" Akron asked.

"Yes, it does. It is the reason we've been working on this computer system in the first place."

Akron's interest was renewed, and he sat upright and listened with enthusiasm. His thoughts were already flitting about to dreams of the glory he might yet achieve.

"The World Council has decided to make one more push to find intelligent life. Most of the community feels that somewhere there has to be intelligent life other than that which developed on Earth and has colonized other planets in the nearby galaxies. But the time and expense involved are too great for small expeditions, except for the robotic probes that are frequently launched."

Akron's frown spoke before he said the words. "But Uncle Horatio, the entire Milky Way Galaxy and all the neighboring galaxies have been searched and no intelligent life has been found. Is this great project just a rehash of what's been done already?"

"No, not a rehash. There are billions of galaxies, Akron, I need not remind you. What we've searched is in comparison to examining a few grains of sand on a beach and deciding that since no life exists in those grains then it doesn't exist on the planet at all."

Horatio rose and walked to a chart that hung down from the ceiling. It was an astronomical map of several galactic clusters that make up the local group of galaxies.

"The Council plans to send a ship on a mission to several clusters of galaxies. More than a ship, really, more like a flying computer, transportation for the Capek-100. But we will include people; hopefully a few dozen volunteers will go aboard, to serve as ambassadors of the human species. They will be put into suspended animation at first. To operate such a ship will take nothing less than the Capek-100, but even it will need refinements, and the programming will take us, if you'll help, the better part of a year."

The professor sat down and looked at his nephew, who was still studying the chart. Akron was basically a good person, Horatio mused, but somehow he's come to believe that fame is what is important in life. Certainly he didn't get that from his father, but being fourth-born in a competitive family probably explains it. This drive for recognition will hurt him someday, or worse, it will hurt others.

"A year of unglamorous work," Horatio added. The statement summed up the basic argument that had already formed in Akron's mind. The young man nodded, but his mind was racing, and had passed by that obvious drawback to getting involved in the project.

"How will it work, uncle? I mean, if everyone is in suspended animation how will they know they've reached a planet with intelligent life?"

"That is the problem for us to solve. I think we can devise a system whereby the Capek's life analysis capabilities can be tied into the life support system, to revive a number of persons who would make the initial exploration."

In the brightness that began to shine in Akron's eyes Horatio saw the cleverness that had made Akron untrustworthy in the eyes of some of his colleagues. Horatio read his nephews thoughts.

"Akron, there won't be any glory in such a mission. Even at the speed of light and quantum jumps it will take years on the ship's clocks, and countless centuries of our time for such a mission to find life. If you consider going, remember that you'd give up all your work here. The only knowledge the inhabited sectors would receive will probably be from probes that the ship will send back."

"Then what's the purpose, if there won't be any contact other than with the people on the ship?"

Horatio shrugged. "It's more philosophical than scientific, I must admit. Humans have spread widely throughout our own galaxy, and for eons to come that will provide room and enough resources. Most people are like you, skeptical of ever finding intelligent life forms other than Homo sapiens. For several centuries now the theologians and philosophers have been returning to the theory that the story of Adam and Eve is literal. So, with interest lagging this might be the last time in the foreseeable future that such a mission can be launched. It's a last-ditch investment in the search for life. We had a difficult time convincing the Council, and we might still fail if the Capek-100 can't handle the computer requirements. That's why I need you."

Wise as he was, even Horatio couldn't see what was formulating in Akron's mind. First, the ambitious youth thought about the capabilities of the Capek-100, named after the ancient inventor of the word 'robot', and the most sophisticated computer system ever devised, advanced even in this society where technology did most of the traditional chores of humans. Then he quickly analyzed the mission's plans and the programming needed to control the life-search functions.

Akron turned to his uncle, "It sounds like a great challenge; I'll be happy to work with you."

Fourteen months passed before all arrangements were completed. Against his uncle's wishes Akron decided to enter into suspended animation and make the trip. None of the one hundred and six passengers had any idea where, or when, they would awaken, or if they would ever return home again. On the day before leaving planetary orbit Akron, in his capacity as assistant programmer, gained access to the master program banks of the Capek-100 and made some final adjustments.

Horatio had mixed feelings knowing he'd likely be long gone before any results from the expedition were known, but also that he wouldn't know if Akron caused any problems for the mission.

Several months of human-calculated time passed on the spaceship Eterna's clocks, and centuries passed on the home planet before the ship approached a galaxy. Sophisticated probes were released and began to search for life readings. Then, according to instructions put into it on the day before departure, the Capek-100 awakened Akron.

When he checked the readouts Akron knew that his program adjustment had worked: the Capek-100 would only awaken him, not several others on an alternating basis each time a galaxy was approached. When life is found I'll be the ambassador, Akron thought, thrilled at his cleverness and foresight.

During the weeks that the Eterna cruised the galaxy awaiting reports from the probes, Akron busied himself writing a diary, studying the ship's engineering, and restudying the Capek's capabilities. Even he was not completely aware of all the intricacies of this incredible machine. By the time life was found, and he had allowed the others to be awakened, his knowledge would give him all the advantage he'd need to control the ship, the personnel, and possibly, a world.

When all the probes had returned no-life readings the Eterna automatically switched directions, made a quantum jump and headed off towards the next nearest galaxy. Bored, Akron had himself put into suspended animation once more. This procedure was repeated several times, and Akron became depressed and lonely. The ship's clocks read twenty-one years, six months, fourteen days.

Akron was just awakening from the suspended state for the tenth time, still in the dazed moments before complete awareness, when he noticed the red danger lights lit all around him, like rows and rows of fire alarms. Confused, he ran, stumbling from chamber to chamber, pounding on the capsules that contained his fellow travelers. He screamed, but in vain, for when there is no life, there is no sound, and Akron was surrounded by the dead, over one hundred capsules of corpses.

Only a determined and ambitious man such as Akron could have maintained his sanity at that point. He busied himself in technical readings, and found what he was searching for in an obscure manual buried in one of the sub-libraries. The Capek-100 confirmed his fears: when Akron had made his program adjustments over twenty-one years ago, he had inadvertently canceled the Capek's Basic Law, that is, that a robot cannot allow a human being to be injured by the robot's own actions, or inactions. The Capek was no longer required to be concerned with the life support systems of anyone but Akron, and stopped monitoring and adjusting the depths of consciousness of the other travelers. Without occasional fine-tuning to the level of suspended animation, the human body would reach a point where revival was not possible.

Loneliness during his conscious hours had not bothered Akron because he had busied himself studying the ship and mentally preparing for his great discovery of non-human intelligent life. Now he experienced loneliness at least equal to that of the first astronauts of many centuries ago. He was afraid to return to the suspended state, though his scientific mind told him that the tragedy had actually proved the safety of the system for him.

For the next couple of months much of Akron's time was spent daydreaming of home, his family, and of his glorious return. His dream was broken by one of the monitor robots. The message was an understatement:

"Have verified existence of Class M life on fourth (4th) planet of Star

System 129, Group 14-A.

Monitoring systems active. Human control

of life search systems is requested."

Life! I've discovered new life! Akron congratulated himself, with a slight

nod to Uncle Horatio, long gone but not quite forgotten. Once again Akron felt

the stirring excitement he'd often experienced when he'd been able to solve a

mathematical problem that no one else could comprehend. He made

preparations to depart the Eterna on a shuttlecraft, first firing off a message

robot to his distant home planet.

As the ancient explorers probably did, Akron exited his landing craft with

an air of superiority, but tinged with a slight sense of foreboding. His confidence

was increased when the inhabitants approached him. They looked human,

though hairier, and were dressed in what appeared to be animal skins. Clearly, I

am more advanced, the explorer thought.

"I come from a distant planet, and am pleased that I have found you,"

greeted Akron, aware that the creatures couldn't possibly understand his worlds,

but hopefully would grasp the meaning.

In a language that was merely noise to Akron, the leader said, "Greetings,

we are glad that we found you."

It was several weeks before enough of each other's language had been learned to enable a conversation to take place.

"Our ancestors came here from a distant land also," said the leader, called Adhamah. "They came in a craft like yours, only much larger."

"I too have a larger ship, up there," said Akron, pointing skyward.

Nodding, Adhamah continued. "I am the direct descendent of the leader, and I must keep the laws that forbid us from building flying craft."

"Why is that?"

Adhamah shrugged. "Our Special Book tells us that our ancestors destroyed their home and all the nearby villages because they fought each other with flying craft and terrible weapons. Our ancestors escaped in one of those flying craft and traveled many years before finding this place."

Akron was torn between disgust that he, with his knowledge of science and with the capabilities of the Eterna, should have discovered only an agrarian and stagnant culture, and ambition at the possibility of leading this culture into the scientific age. He could be the most famous person in this world, at least!

It is one thing to be a leader of people who want a leader; it is another to have the power and the ability to lead people who don't care one way or the other, and will ignore your attempts to lead them. At first the natives tried to appease Akron by listening to his grand schemes and plans for the future. When he persisted in trying to implement changes in their primitive farming methods they quietly, but stubbornly, resisted. Soon they ignored Akron. They showed not the slightest interest anymore in his tales of the adventurers and colonists of his own galaxy.

So Akron went back to the mother ship Eterna, reset the automatic pilot and again went into suspended animation. His last conscious thoughts were of the tumultuous welcome he would receive upon his return home.

Another two decades or so of traditional time transpired while Akron slept. The Eterna, her innards a complex mechanism of millions of micro dots controlled by the always alert Capek-100, sped resolutely toward its home planet, a speck so far away the distance was incomprehensible to the human mind.

Even a math-oriented mind such as Akron's could not have calculated the time that would pass on his home planet while the Eterna flew at light speeds with many quantum jumps. Human knowledge of math and physics had never been able to determine exactly the time differential when a body traveled at light speed, attempting to defy basic laws of physics, and also to make quantum leaps through areas of empty space, which, in effect, defeated the restrictions of the speed of light.

"It gets very complicated even for me," Horatio use to say, then he would admit, "I don't think it's possible to for us to make exact calculations, since any speed faster than light cannot be precisely measured by our instruments." And certainly Akron could not have imagined that centuries after the Eterna left, survivors of a galactic war would escape the dying Milky Way in a ship even faster than the Eterna and find a suitable planet to live on in a very, very distant corner of the universe.

Since he didn't know this, he hadn't programmed the Capek-100 to specifically awaken him when it reached the home planet—-only to awaken him as before, when intelligent life was detected

The Milky Way was a dark galaxy when the Eterna returned to it. What planets remained were cold cinders, her civilizations long destroyed or abandoned, cities now dead outposts of the humanity that once flourished. Capek-100 searched for life, found none, and set out to look elsewhere. Akron slept on, and on, and on, and dreamt of his fame.

Here is another short, and true, story, of those growing up days when the simplest pleasures were the best. We had fun, even without video games and without someone organizing all our activities. --erw

The Field

The flames of the fire flickered upward and specks of orange mingled with the stars that dotted the sky. Dark gray smoke also rose, and with it the musty smell of blackening potatoes. The boys moved closer to the fire as the frosty air cut through their windbreakers. It was late autumn, and they were in Kaiser Field--the playground, ballpark, and campfire grounds for the neighborhood kids.

The field stretched for two city blocks between a row of houses and the fence of a steel company, and was about 150 yards wide. Where the fence ended, and across the railroad tracks that ran alongside it, George Lake began. While the specific name 'Kaiser Field' (its origin a mystery) referred to a clearing where kids played baseball, the older boys had ventured farther and extended the boundaries of their playground the length of the field, to the lake, and to the woodsy area beyond.

This wasn't a gigantic area, but when you are twelve years old It Is a universe unto itself. The western end edged up to George Lake, a body of water that was somewhere between a large pond and a small lake. On its shores grew cattails, which we harvested each year, dried out in our attics, and then 'smoked' the following summer, mainly as a mosquito deterrent.

George Lake wasn't very deep. You could almost walk across it except that you might get stuck in its squishy, muddy bottom. So we would build a raft, or borrow Big Mike's rowboat (without him knowing it) and row across the lake with our sleeping bags and other camping gear. We would spend the night roasting hot dogs and marshmallows and telling outlandish ghost stories, and hardly sleep at all.

The other end of the field abutted St. Al's parish hall. There was also a St. Al's church, a St. Al's school, and a St. Al's nunnery. It was here that I went to school from kindergarten until the eight grade, and where I served many a mass at the church. And it was here that Father Henry would grab me—and other wayward altar boys—by the short hairs around the ears, to remind us that we had screwed up at mass, by laughing or garbling our Latin prayers. But he was a great guy; he would have made a good father—well, he was a *Father,* but he would have made a good father.

And it was here that one of my best friends, Beans—his name was Larry but his nickname was Beans; don't ask why, it's too complicated to explain— would scare the young fourth grade altar boys. It seems that every week there was a funeral. This was an old parish and there were lots of old people, and someone was always dying. Beans and I served at many a funeral service, usually on a Friday afternoon, which was neat because we got out of school for an hour our so.

Well, you know, you have to train the new guys coming along so we'd include a youngster to break him in. The service at the funeral home was almost always an open casket. Beans had this way about him where he starts whispering; telling the neophyte to look over at the casket.

"I think he's moving," Beans would say.

"Yeah, he blinked," I would add.

One of these poor little guys peed his pants he was so sure that the corpse was going to stand up and join us in the Hail Mary.

But I digress; I was talking about the field. Thinking back now, I realize how lucky we were to enjoy the advantages of open spaces, woods, and lakes while growing up in such a densely populated region as northwest Indiana. Our town actually abutted the border of Illinois and the city limits of Chicago. But there were acres of woods and fields that to inquisitive young boys became vast, uncharted worlds.

Early every spring greenery sprouted almost overnight. Young elms and a variety of bushes and weeds decorated the edges of the field, but the trampling of young boys prevented anything from growing very large in the center. In fact, the combination of boys crashing through and over, winds blowing across nearby Lake Michigan and the snow and ice of winter usually leveled each year's growth.

The exception was Old John's Place, where a couple dozen ancients oaks maintained a foothold they had gained in some long ago era. These, plus John's animal coop, cut the field into two sections.

Often my brother and I would throw corn kernels through the wire fence of the coop. Slopping through the mud to get the corn, the ducks and chickens would wake the cats dozing on the roof of the coop. The mongrel dogs that also lived there would awaken too, and the quacks, barks, and trombone-like honks of geese would echo throughout the field and into the nearby homes. A stranger might think he was near a farm, yet we lived in the shadows and smells of the great steel and oil refineries of the Calumet Region.

Past John's coop, the part of the field closest to the lake was brown and dusty, with piles of broken concrete and asphalt giving the appearance of a bombed city. Years ago this area had been alive with green frogs, brown toads, chattering crickets, fireflies, and ten-foot-high bulrushes amidst a brackish bottom that was more a heavy dampness than a body of water. Dumping by street repair crews had taken away our jungle and given us the bombed city in which we played 'army.'

To the field I took our Sheltie, Prince, to romp and smell the smells that he found nowhere else in the neighborhood. Two hundred times, three hundred; how many times I walked with him, knowing that when I got him home I'd have to brush out the sticker and weed collection he'd brought home caught in his fur.

By late autumn the trees were bare of leaves and the field was brown and gray and chilly. Here we gathered for that great tradition, the Thanksgiving Day touch football game. After awhile the football game couldn't compete with the aromas of roast turkey and stuffing and pumpkin pie which enticed us back to the warmth and flavors of our homes.

As much as we enjoyed the field during the daytime for baseball, football, and exploration, sunset brought an even greater thrill: the darkness. Darkness so black that where the sky ended and the ground began could not be distinguished until you had gained your 'night eyes'.

My younger brother and his buddies were gathered around the fire, talking, laughing, and waiting for the potatoes. It was winter, and roasting potatoes was just an excuse to be out there, for the real fun was in the crackling fire, the camaraderie, the mysterious, silent darkness. The boys stamped their feet and pulled hats down over their heads to ward off the chill.

Quietly I crawled over the snow-encrusted ground until I was close enough to hear the conversation. Then I began to toss snowballs into the group. Startled, they looked around, but after staring into the fire they were nearly blind when looking out into the dark, and could not see me though I was only a few yards away. Some of the snowballs sizzled in the flames as I continued my barrage.

Just when they were about to abandon their camp, just a bit frightened, my brother, suspicious, called my name, hoping it was me, and not some of the meaner, older boys. I stifled a laugh.

"Hey, is that you?" he said, hoping it was so. "Hey, cut it out!"

No longer able to contain my laughter, I stood up and showed myself. The boys were so relieved that it was only me that they didn't even retaliate with a snowball bombardment of their own.

Mike, my younger, chubby brother, offered me a potato as I joined the group around the dying fire. I picked up a stick off the ground, stabbed a crisp, almost blackened potato, and bit into it. It was delicious. The wind gusted across the open field and forced us closer to the fire.

Even today I'll eat the entire skin of a baked potato and invariably remember those day and nights in the field.

No need to read too much into this story. I just always thought dragons were kind of neat and probably misunderstood. Well, I suppose our hero, Reyneld, is rather naïve. But still, one must be careful not to be too quick to look for trouble. And remember what Pogo said.--erw

The Last Dragon

Atop a hill that overlooked the castle the dragon kept watch. Just before the sun had appeared over the horizon but after the first rays of morning had already painted the sky, the knight rode out across the drawbridge. The dragon perked its nostrils, puffed steam, and breathed deeply. The knight galloped steadily forward, his lance in his hand and his sword at his side. Maybe today, he thought, I will finish my family's work.

For years the knights and dragons had done battle. For generations, actually, and neither this knight nor his father could remember when knights and dragons had not been enemies.

"It is our duty, our destiny," Sir Randle told his son. "And it was my father's duty, and his father's, and so it shall be yours, and your son's, too."

The young boy had a bad habit: he often asked questions for which there were no easy answers.

"Why do we fight the dragons, father?"

"We have always fought the dragons, son. To protect the farmers, the travelers in the countryside, our towns. Without us to defend the towns they would be burned to a cinder by the hot breath of the dragon-beasts."

Sir Randle looked proudly at his son, sure that the freckled youngster would gallantly carry forward the honor of the House of Halenault, famous throughout the realm as dragon-slayers for many generations. The red-haired boy was also proud—-of his heritage and of his father, and he longed to ride in quest of dragons.

"It is the noblest calling, to seek out the dragons."

"Do you think there will be any dragons left for me to slay by the time I am ready?"

Sir Randle shrugged his shoulders. "I'm sure there will be, lad. These hills and valleys are filled with the monsters. They hide in caves and lakes and no one knows how many there are. Our towns will never be safe until the last beast is destroyed, but I'm sure that won't happen before you've done battle with them."

"What do they look like, father?"

"Ah, what magnificent creatures they are! With their blood red eyes shining in the night sky, and the wind whipped into a fury by their huge, flapping wings! The sight of them sends a shiver down the spine of any God-fearing person! And their size alone; huge, terrifying giants; that alone can freeze a body with fear! Some of them are larger than our entire castle."

"Oh surely, father, they couldn't be that big, could they?"

"Yes, lad, believe it. Some of the older ones are that large. You know, a dragon never stops growing, so a very old one can be gigantic."

Sir Randle's voice trailed off and his eyes glazed as he looked upward, searching for a speck in the sky that would slowly grow until its shadow covered the town square.

"And then the fire," he said softly.

"The what, father?"

"The fire," he repeated, louder and with terror in his voice.

"Fire like you've never believed could exist outside of Hell itself. Red, orange, yellow, even blue fire, and green, white, all colors, any colors, as if the beast was taunting us with brilliance, only to use those fiery hues to incinerate towns, homes, castles, and people. Ah yes, my boy, many brave knights have died in the battles, and many more will."

Sir Randle held his son around the shoulders with his huge hands. He was a big man in both fame and appearance. Legends of Sir Randle's duels with fierce, fire-breathing dragons had made his name famous throughout the land, as was expected of the great grandson of the beloved Sir Howard of Halenault.

"You must grow to be a strong knight, my son. You must practice the art of battle, and keep proud the family crest."

The son was eager that his time to hunt dragons would come soon, before they were all slain. None had been seen in his lifetime, although occasionally a story from some distant land would be told by travelers, but no one knew of a town being burned by dragons in recent memory.

One day the boy, now a young man, asked his father, "How did men and dragons become enemies?"

A quizzical look crawled over the bearded face of Sir Randle.

"Why, it's always been that way. It's the nature of things. Just as men and unicorns were always friends, men and dragons have always been enemies." He dotted his explanation with a sharp nod of his head.

"What happened to the unicorns? I have never seen a unicorn either."

Sir Randle shook his head slowly. "Ah, a sad fate. Food for the dragons."

"Oh, how awful!"

"The poor creatures were too trusting, too timid. They didn't run away, or attempt to fight. They just stood and watched and the dragons flew down upon them with breath afire, singeing the air and destroying whole herds of the beautiful creatures in one fell swoop. Your grandfather could have told you about that. Myself, I never saw it happen, but by all that is righteous, such horror is reason enough to slay dragons!"

So the young man grew up and practiced how to fight. He learned about the habits of dragons, of their power, and how to destroy them. He learned that it is best to attack early in the morning, when the dragon's breath is frosty with the night air. Then a knight could move in and thrust his lance into the dragon's heart, for only into the heart could a fatal wound be delivered.

It seems unfair, somehow, the young man thought. Here I am, sixteen summers old, and I've yet to see a dragon, but I keep practicing how to kill dragons for when I do see one.

"Father, would it be possible for men and dragons to live together peaceably, without fearing one another?"

Had he been younger, Sir Randle would have grabbed his son and shaken understanding into the lad. But, older now, he simply sighed before speaking.

"Son, once an enemy, always an enemy. A dragon is an enemy of man. It is nature. And it is man's nature to slay dragons. Without the knights to search out and destroy dragons, the towns, the women, the children could never be safe. We have to go out and destroy our enemies wherever they may be. And we must maintain honor, for without honor man is no better than the beasts themselves."

The young man was not satisfied, but he was not used to arguing with his father. He commented politely: "Father, there may not even be any more dragons. No one has seen one in years and there have been no reports of travelers being attacked, or towns burned. The dragons may be all dead."

"Son, dragons live a long time, as I have told you. Years are nothing to the monsters. We must be sure. The dragons may be hiding in the deep forests. Remember your duty and remember your honor. I know that other young men are following different pursuits, fighting wars in distant lands, searching for mythical treasures, but you are of the House of Halenault. Do not forget that!"

With his graying mass of hair and beard, clear blue eyes, his stature, and deep voice, Sir Randle was an impressive looking man. Many knights had followed him into battle not knowing who they would be fighting, but only because Sir Randle's courage spread among them and made them eager to follow. Now Sir Randle's son, the last knight of the House of Halenault, famous dragon-slayers, would go forth to protect the townspeople.

When he was mature and well versed in the ways of combat the son of Sir Randle went out of the castle, reluctantly. His friends were adventuring in faraway lands. But the son of Sir Randle must go in quest of dragons, though the eagerness of childhood was waning. He was not sure where he was going, but all his life he had been reminded of his duty, so now he went out to do it.

Hidden among the trees on the hill the dragon lifted off his quarters to get a better look at his adversary. The dragon knew the time would have to come; knew that sooner or later one more knight would search him out to do battle, to perform courageously, but foolishly; for the dragon could not be defeated.

The dragon had never been defeated, never in all the years that men had stuffed themselves into the clumsy armor and rode out gallantly to the cheers of the people, some to return with boastful claims of tremendous battles with huge, fire-breathing monsters, to be adored by the people and esteemed from then on as a great warrior. And never did these knights go out in further quests; afterward they were given more honors than duties. What duties a knight had after having faced the dragon were tutorial and ceremonial. Jousting in tournaments, escorting the princess, that sort of thing. And what happens when men are honored for deeds that no one has seen, but lives only in the tales of the men themselves? The stories, naturally, become exaggerations many times over. The dragons become bigger, their breath hotter, their teeth sharper, their danger to mankind overwhelming. So overwhelming do the dragons become that no knight is expected to make more than one quest. Such a tradition no doubt emerged subtly from the knights' own tales.

The dragon knew he could not be defeated, and he knew the tales that the knights told and how false they were. Oh, he understood. After all, what brave knight would come back and admit that he not only had not slain a dragon, but that the dragon was not a danger? What purpose would the knight serve then, if there were no need for dragon-slayers? Though the tales became exaggerated, what knight would come out and tell the true story of his encounter with the dragon? Such a story would surely not be believed.

The dragon watched as the young knight headed out of the castle on his white steed in the direction of the hill. Traditionally, the knights would ride to the top of this hill, turn to salute the castle, and then ride on, unerringly led by the spirit of their forefathers in the direction of the dragon's lair. And the dragon knew that just as he was invincible, he would always be found. So there was no great need to hide from the knight. Still, the dragon abhorred the eventual meeting and wanted to delay it as long as he could. So he spread his leathery wings and rose into the sky, gracefully, not screeching at all, as men would describe his flight. How would this knight describe his meeting with the dragon?

How many dragons would he claim to have slain, and how many more knights would come out of the castle before the dragon would be allowed to rest?

Feeling no enmity for anyone or anything, Reyneld, son of Sir Randle, searched for dragons. Mostly he enjoyed the scenery and the time to be alone with his thoughts. He realized that he didn't really fear dragons. He'd been taught to, but it was hard for him to fear something he only knew from songs and tales of boastful knights. He believed in dragons, of course, he just wasn't sure they were all that dangerous. It seemed that a lot people told a lot of stories, but did very little. There were stories in town these days about great treasures that were taken in the latest battles against some distant and ruthless enemy. But Reyneld couldn't understand why these people were a threat. Just as he wasn't sure how dragons that were never seen could be a threat; or, if they were so dangerous, how he alone was going to stop them.

For many months Reyneld followed the trail of the dragon. He wasn't sure how he followed it, he just seemed to go instinctively. One night, after almost a year of searching and living off the land, Reyneld stopped near a quiet brook. The water hardly moved at all, just enough to send a bubbly song into the wind. Across the brook, which was about thirty feet wide but no more than a few inches deep at any point, was a forest of dark trees. As entrancing as was the scene at the brook, with the singing water and accompanying birds, that's how mysterious the woods appeared. Somehow Reyneld knew, felt, that the dragon's lair was near. Early tomorrow he would meet the object of his quest.

The knight slept fitfully. He was fully awake long before the sun rose, and in the chilly darkness he crossed the brook, the only sound the gentle splish-splash of his horse stepping through the shallow water. On the other side of the brook he stopped for a moment and stared at the wall of dark trees that was the edge of the forest. He would have to find the dragon soon, while it still slept. Reyneld went forward into the forest, pulling back on his horse so that it stepped softly on the leaves and branches on the forest floor. First light was approaching when he saw it. Against the side of a mound in a grove of young oaks lay the dragon!

It was the largest animal Reyneld had ever seen. In the darkness it would have been hard to distinguish the animal from the mound of dirt, except for the spike-like protuberances all along the back and tail, a tail that stretched out many yards from the bulk of the body. The spikes appeared to be covered with forest moss. The knight was fascinated and stood there for several minutes admiring the beast, knowing he should strike before it awoke, but too engrossed in admiration to move. Finally the nervous horse began to stamp its feet and jarred the knight into action.

Reyneld alit from the horse and approached the dragon with lance in hand. With luck one thrust of his weapon would finish this splendid beast. Then, an eye appeared. A blood-red eyeball. The knight froze. Suddenly the beast sprang up from its slumber, more agile than the forest cats. The neck and head

rose higher and higher into the air while that tail waved back and forth,

scrapping away rocks and bushes and rolling them aside as if they were paper. A

gaping hole developed in the head and out of the hole came a red appendage,

forked, slithering like some gargantuan snake searching for shade from the noon

sun. Reyneld, still several feet from the beast, feared that the tongue itself could

reach him. Glimmering teeth appeared, pointed and white, whiter than a bucket

of fresh milk. Both eyes stared unblinking at the knight; two pools of blood

examining an intruder that had violated the sanctuary of the forest. Steam issued

from the mouth and the flaring nostrils, black wells that were large enough to

engulf the knight, or so they looked to the terrified hunter. All that training for

naught, Reyneld thought. I know I must attack now, yet I also know that I am

paralyzed by awe and fear. Such a fantastic beast! How did the others manage

to slay such creatures without being awestruck? These thoughts went through

Reyneld's mind as he awaited his death, for there was no doubt he would die,

whether from a swat of the spiked tail or from the crunch of the razor-sharp

teeth didn't matter. He only wanted to absorb more of this wonder in his mind's

eye before his demise. As yet the dragon had not completely risen; it half sat on

the ground, but already it towered above the knight. Reyneld estimated that its

head was as far above the ground as the height of four men standing on top of

each other.

The dragon hissed, which startled Reyneld into the first movement he'd made since the eyeball appeared. Then a flame shot out of the cavern that was a mouth, engulfing the ground and the trees around Reyneld, but not harming the knight at all. The charred ground and the smoking tree branches shook Reyneld. Maybe it was the realization that he should be dead but wasn't that gave him the motivation. He charged the dragon and with all his strength hurled his lance at the heart of the beast. The weapon sunk into the scaly skin and went on through, coming out against the hillside. No wound could Reyneld see. The dragon picked up the lance with a clawed forefoot and snapped it into many bits, then brushed the pieces away while hissing forth a cloud of hot steam. Reyneld backed away, his eyes large with amazement, his mind too impressed to be scared anymore.

Then a really strange thing happened: the dragon spoke!

"You are a young one. The youngest I've seen. It took you a long time to find me." It was a harsh voice, as one would expect from a very old and very wise wizard.

Reyneld was dumbstruck, a helpless stand of flesh and bones and puny armor in the shadow of this incredible power.

"You had to find me, of course," the dragon continued, "because you were convinced I existed. Actually I'm not real, which is why your lance didn't harm me. I don't exist, hence you can't kill me. But I can kill you because you believe I'm real."

Still speechless with wonder, Reyneld sat down on the ground and listened to a dragon's tale that even in an age of myths was fantastic.

The dragon explained how men had hunted him, or beasts like him, for centuries, never to slay him, but to brag. Now men were busy fighting wars and conquering countries and bragging about those feats. In some places they were searching for mythical cities of gold and jewels. They did not have the time or interest for dragons anymore. Only a few myths persisted, just enough to keep one dragon around. He was the last dragon, here because men had bid him to be here, and he would be around while there were men who believed in him.

Finally Reyneld spoke. "You mean you only exist as a dream of men?"

"Something like that. Men must have something to conquer to prove their courage and bravery. So they imagine dangerous beasts that must be destroyed; enemies to defeat never realizing that they are their own worst enemy."

"But what about the stories of battles with dragons, villages burned, and the adventures of the knights? My father is a great dragon slayer!"

The dragon rolled his eyes. "What do you expect a trained, pampered knight to say when he returns, knowing what the people want to hear? That he met a talking dragon that wasn't really *real*? Actually, the ones that returned probably believed they had performed some feat of bravery.

"At first many knights were slain as we, the dragons, tried to prove the folly of fighting something that exists only in one's mind. We did terrorize a few travelers; after all, dragons get bored, too, waiting around for a knight to come charging at us with a lance aimed at the heart. But people are stubborn, and some of the knights were very stupid. We tried to hide, to avoid contact; but we found that if men want to find something to fight, they'll find it. All it does is avoid facing up to real problems."

"What could be more important than facing up to our enemies and keeping our towns safe?" asked Reyneld.

"Safe from what? If you didn't fight each other you could spend more time growing and learning and building. If you didn't waste time hunting make-believe monsters you could be out hunting for food or growing fruit. Ah, well, it's almost over."

"What do you mean? What's almost over?"

The dragon shifted his weight, brushing against a tree, which sent it crashing to the ground. A few birds squawked but the dragon ignored the commotion.

"As I said, men are finding other battles to fight, other things to brag about. Some things won't really change, but as men become more cynical they'll quit believing in monsters. They'll still hunt other, helpless beasts with their weapons. But I'll be gone because men won't believe in dragons anymore. You're probably the last knight who will come looking for me. That's good."

"What shall I say when I return to the castle? Should I say that you are no danger to the people, and that I talked to you?"

"You know what the other knights have said. You have a chance to change that though I doubt if anyone would believe you. They would laugh and scorn you. I guess it doesn't matter because men will keep finding battles to fight. That's what so frustrating." Again the dragon rolled his eyes upward, the dragon form of sighing.

"And where will you go? What happens to dragons when men don't believe in them anymore?"

"It depends. Dragons can still exist, but how they'll exist depends on how people think of them. If you want to believe in harmless, lovable dragons, I can manage that. Remember, knight, the world around you will be as you believe it to be. Now go, for I grow weary of people."

The dragon rose to his full height on all four legs and unfolded wings that blocked the light of the morning sun. He puffed great clouds of steam and with a graceful leap was sky borne. In seconds he was a mere speck in the sky. Reyneld watched amidst the leaves swirled about by the wind of the dragon's flight.

Reyneld returned to his castle after a sojourn in the forest. He was greeted by his father, who was ill and could walk only with the aid of a staff, and several of the townsfolk. They were eager to hear Reyneld's stories of adventure.

Reyneld walked to the center of the town square and waited until the buzz of voices had died down. He held up a hand and spoke to them of he places he had visited. Then he said:

"Fear no more the dragon. I have slain the last dragon."

The crowd cheered wildly only to be interrupted by another knight, one who had come to the town recently from another kingdom.

"Quiet!" this knight commanded.

"This young knight is certainly brave, but he speaks too eagerly. There are many dangers out beyond the limits of the castle walls. Enemies and beasts lurk, waiting for us to drop our guard. I will protect this town if I am given a few strong knights to assist me."

Reyneld tried to dispute the new knight, but to no avail. The people wanted to be scared and they wanted someone to take care of them, so they made the new knight their protector and gave him a fine home and all the food he could eat and once in awhile he went out with his men and they came back with tales of great deeds they had accomplished.

Reyneld's father died shortly thereafter and Reyneld left the town to find a new home where he need not be afraid of legends.

An anecdote from my travels in Europe in 1977...

not for the squeamish.--erw

Bullfights

In Madrid I thought I should go to see the bullfights. Not that I'm a fan; bullfighting always sounded like an awful sport, the torture of a dumb brute of an animal. Still, they were going to have them whether I approved or not, so I'm here, let's go see.

At my hotel I met a honeymooning couple from Lebanon, George and Lisette. We had dinner and did some sightseeing together. They insisted on my joining them...I certainly wouldn't push myself on a couple on their honeymoon!

"The trouble with Spain," George said in a thick accent, "is that not enough English is spoken here."

George was tall, dark and handsome. Lisette was a stunning, dark-eyed, glowing bride. Her English wasn't as good as George's, but she was fluent in French, and I tried to make conversation with the few words I'd picked up while traveling in France just the week before.

"She doesn't understand a word you're saying," said George. "I encourage her to speak English as much as she can so that she will get better at it."

At dinner Saturday night George suggested we go to the bullfights the next day, something I had intended to do anyway, but hadn't expected to have company.

"If you want to get the full flavor of Spain, you must see the bullfights. It is the national sport, you know," George lectured.

"They kell the bull, no?" asked Lisette.

"Ah, my dear, it is a grand sport, I am told, with much color, music, pageantry!" But George admitted he'd never seen a bullfight before and was mainly curious, as I was.

On Sunday we went in George's rented car. He had already purchased tickets for the 'sombra' section, that is, in the shade, as opposed to the cheaper seats in the 'sol' section. The stadium was more circular than the oval stadiums I was used to, and of course there was sand instead of grass. As we waited in our seats, my program, written in choppy English, told me that if one was not in his seat early, he might not find his seat until after the first bull was killed, missing a 'nice part of the performance.'

"See George, it says write here that it's nice. I'm sure the bulls won't mind at all." He didn't seem to quite grasp my sense of humor.

George then read this part of the program to Lisette, but she sat quietly, unsmiling. Last night she was happy and laughing, drinking champagne as we visited several clubs. But I don't think today's activity was one she had listed on her honeymoon schedule.

Promptly at five-thirty the event began. Colorful matadors and their assistants entered in parade, like living works of art, some strutting proudly, others on horseback. The bright costumes were a delight to the eye. There were yellow and pink costumes, blue, purple, black and gold, violet, white and gold, blazing red, and numerous combinations, all embroidered with gold and silver.

After the paraders had cleared the arena, the president of the bullfights waved a white cloth and to the sound of trumpets a gate opened and an angry, bewildered bull charged into the ring. Pedro Ruiz, the matador, studied the bull's quickness and temperament, then approached with a calmness I found admirable. He faced the bull with only his yellow and purple cape. With a series of flourishes he tantalized the bull, which without fail charged at the hypnotic cape only to be frustrated by the smooth movements of the matador.

"Do you thenk the bulls are drugged to make them less dangerous?" Lisette asked George.

"No, they are dangerous, but not too smart. The bull is attracted by the motion of the cape. Watch the matador and you'll see that he stands nearly still, but he flutters the cape, and that's what the bull charges."

Next, the picadors entered the ring. There were two of them, astride heavily padded and blindfolded horses. The riders carried long pikes. Several of the assistants drew the bull towards one of the picadors, and the harassed animal finally charged at the horse. The skillful rider controlled the horse with one hand while with the other he thrust the pike into the nape of the bull.

Some of the spectators cheered at the first sight of blood as it spat into the air, landing on the rider's leg, on the sand, and on the head of the bull. I'll admit I was startled, and Lisette stifled an "Ohh!"

The wound didn't seem to bother the bull, who attacked the horse with renewed ferocity. Three times the bull was punished with sharp blows of the pike. The blood did not spurt as before, but seeped out indecently from both sides of the bull, the beginning of a certain and unavoidable death.

Despite the wound, death was a ways off yet. The matador returned, this time with the short darts called banderillas. Pedro Ruiz approached the bull head-on, without a cape, but with a banderilla in each hand, arms upraised and darts pointed down towards the shoulders of the beast. Taunting the bull by feinting thrusts of the darts, Ruiz eventually goaded it into charging. Gracefully, with bare inches to spare, the matador sidestepped the charge, at the same time piercing the bull with the darts.

I glanced at Lisette; she seemed awed, and couldn't take her eyes off the fight, (if you could call it a fight). Her hand still rested covering her mouth, as if she knew another cry of shock would be forthcoming if she watched long enough. Is it the attraction of horror that brought us and thousand of others to this, I wondered?

The famous red cape came next, as the matador again went into a series of flourishing passes at the weakened bull. Only now it was an obvious prelude to death; the imagery of the original series of flourishes, that here was a genuine battle of brute strength versus intelligent bravery and grace, was gone now as the bull's charges became feebler, lacking spirit and power, lacking the potential to win the duel. With every move the bull's wounds were irritated, and blood stained the sand, while the crowd yelled, "Ole!" with each charge at the indomitable matador.

Now Pedro Ruiz pulled the sword out from under the red cape and held it in his right hand, pointed squarely at the shoulder blades of the bull. With the cape in his left hand he spurred one more charge out of the bull, and then sank the sword about half-way into the stunned beast. The matador and the crowd were disappointed; they had wanted a clean, one-thrust kill. With a shorter sword Ruiz approached the bull, surely in complete shock, and mercifully ended the drama with a prick in the nape. The bull dropped to its knees as if shot, then slowly fell over on its side. It was dead.

"Exciting, no?" said George. Lisette smiled politely, I nodded uncertainly. "Rather brutal", I said, to say something.

"The bull is bred for this," explained George. "He knows nothing else but to attack. He is a mad, mindless beast, with no other purpose. It is his fate." He shrugged. I think he was trying to convince himself as well as Lisette.

Three more fights passed with little comment among us. One exceptionally feisty bull received cheers from the crowd and the matador enhanced his reputation by toying with it for a while longer before finishing the job. This bull had fought mightily, charging repeatedly like a runaway locomotive, and had never quit until it was thoroughly drained of strength, bleeding and ferocious until its inevitable demise.

I figured then that for a bull to leave the ring alive was rarer than a perfect game in baseball. The other two bulls were meek in comparison, making only minimal resistance, as if they knew their fate and did not want to glamorize the slaughter by making it more fun for the crowd.

I wasn't sure I wanted to sit through the entire card, which was six fights. But George had the car and I was sort of stuck. I began to doubt I'd have much of an appetite for dinner, which we had planned to celebrate our last day in Madrid.

The fifth bull was a huge, excited beast. Several times he almost caught the matador off guard with sudden charges. His attacks on the horses were vicious. One picador was thrown off his horse and was saved from serious injury only because several assistants ran out to divert the bull. The crowd cheered in appreciation of bravery and courage on both sides. I had to admit that this was exciting. I certainly didn't want anyone to get hurt, but I couldn't help rooting for the bull to put on such a good struggle that its life would be spared.

The bull continued to give the matador, one Jose Menez, a difficult time, finally catching him on the leg and knocking him to the ground. Again, alert assistants distracted the bull while the matador escaped and received first aid. Gallantly he returned to the ring, to the wild applause of the aficionados. Now, to prove himself, he had to fight the bull with his cape for longer than the usual time, and often approached closer to the bull than appeared prudent.

To cap his performance, the injured matador expertly killed the bull with one sure thrust, the sword entering to the hilt. The crowd roared wildly. They threw hats, flowers, and bota bags as the victorious matador circled the ring, proudly displaying his blood-splattered costume, his montera raised in salute to the crowd. This went on for several minutes. Meanwhile a team of mules came out, halters were attached to the dead bull, and it was dragged in the dust. But then the president waved a blue cloth, and in acknowledgment of its courage the bull was first dragged around the ring before being hauled off to wherever they haul dead bulls to. Such an honor!

"It's hard for the bull to win," I said, sarcastically. I hoped George would suggest we leave now, but he was silent.

"Seen enough, George?"

"Oh, no, only one more. Let's stay. I want to see this; there is much bravery on display, much courage."

So I resigned myself to one more fight. I gazed around at the other people, as I really was tired of watching these contests. The last one was a sloppy fight. The matador was young and inexperienced, and could not kill the bull with his sword, or with the descabeloo, the shorter sword. After ten minutes he was given a warning. Supposedly, after three warnings, the matador is not allowed to continue, to his disgrace. Back to the minor leagues, I wondered?

What followed was brutal. Jab after jab, the matador struck the bull, but it would not die. The animal lay hunched over on its front knees, breathing heavily, blood flowing from its nape and shoulders, staining the sand a dull, dark brown. People began to leave; the fights were over, and the death of this last bull was sure and insignificant. It was not unlike fans leaving in the eight inning of a 9-2 baseball game.

Different places, different peoples, different cultures. But I will never understand how such wonderful writers as Hemingway and Michener could be enthralled by this awful ceremony.

This is another baseball story, but this is one is true. Even the names have not been changed!--erw

The Game

It would be the last, and the most important, baseball game of the season. Summer was rapidly changing to autumn and our interests would soon turn from baseball to football, basketball, and Halloween.

Beans, Nose, Sack, Ox, me, and the rest of the team arrived at Clark Field on our green bicycles, our usual form of transportation. Sack spun his wheels, spraying cinders to announce his arrival, on time for a change. The Ers were already there, confidently joking and tossing frayed baseballs around. Their team captain, who wore a 'Tigers' t-shirt that had lost it first three letters, cackled at us.

"C'mon, let's get started so we can beat you guys and go home!"

"Where's your hurry to get home, your momma waitin' for you with cookies and milk?" yelled back Sack.

One reason for the Ers' confidence was that their team had an advantage over us: they cheated.

It didn't have to be blatant. But they took advantage of our eagerness for a game by insisting that they always win the close calls. In any friendly sandlot game the "Safe!" and "Out!" "Fair!" or "Foul!" calls tend to balance out. If one team won a close call the next one, by unwritten law, went to the other team.

"That's foul for sure this time!"

"OK, Sack, get in there and hit it fair this time."

Sack hit a lot of foul balls. He could pull an intentional walk down the left field line. The 'five fouls and you're out' rule was invented because of him.

We didn't mind too much that they took advantage of us because we were rabid baseball fans, and any game was a good game. Some were just better than others. The Ers were different. They'd quit, claim victory, and go home rather than lose an argument, and they knew we'd eventually give in just so the game could continue.

Nose, whose nickname needed no explanation, was our team captain, but we took our team name from Sack's sweatshirt. It spelled U T C A A, for Union Tank Car Athletic Association. We pronounced it 'Utcaa', as a word, not as initials.

Nose fancied himself as our best hitter. (In later years he would fancy himself a ladies' man at Clark High School). Actually I was the best hitter, and Nose, who kept an accurate scorebook of all our games, reluctantly agreed with the statistics, which showed me as our team's biggest run-producer. I had lost the home run title this summer, however, to Sack, who had grown a lot and could hit the ball a long way when he got it into the air. But he often struck out and was too lazy to run when he hit a routine grounder. And he was as likely to hit five fouls and be called out, as he was to hit a home run.

Our teams had evenly split the many games we'd played this summer, so this contest had been mutually agreed upon as 'The Championship'. This was our World Series. And somehow I knew that this would be the last summer of these games. Oh, we'd still play occasionally, maybe. But by next year we'd be in high school, working summer jobs, learning to drive, and the patterns of our activities would change. I could feel this change starting already, and with it a feeling of anticipation and sadness. It chilled me, like the early winter fog rolling in over Lake Michigan. Of course I was too young and naive to begin to understand about such monumental changes that occur at different stages of a person's life. For now though, they could wait.

The game progressed predictably; a run here, two runs there, but with the Ers maintaining a lead that became seemingly insurmountable at 10-2. But we rallied in the fifth inning for six runs to make it close. I'd been having a great game, lot good it did if we lost. In the seventh inning we began another rally. With the Ers ahead by only one run, I reached second base on a scorching line drive to left-centerfield. I slid in ahead of the throw and hugged the base--a piece of paper weighted down with pebbles-- even as the Ers' shortstop tried to shove me off. He tossed the ball to the pitcher and Sack took his place in the batter's box.

As the Ers' pitcher got set on the mound I took my lead. Suddenly the shortstop dashed over and tagged me! He had another ball in his pocket!

"Hidden ball trick, dummy!" he laughed.

"You can't use two balls. He's got the game ball in his glove," I yelled back, pointing to the pitcher. I was furious and wouldn't leave the base even when my teammates told me to give up the fight. But when the Ers said they'd quit, and began to leave the field, I gave in to their treachery, and our rally was over.

We still trailed, by 12-10, going into the bottom of the ninth inning; our last chance. Nose led off with a sharply hit single. Beans did the same, and as my teammates screamed encouragement I stepped up to the plate, imagining myself as Stan Musial. My pride and reputation were on the line. I enjoyed being the kid who got the big hits. I'd done it often, and didn't have to brag because the rest of the gang, and the other team, knew it. But today my most memorable feat was to get picked off base!

When I swung at the first pitch the memory of this game was engraved forever in the history of the 'Green Bicycle Gang.' No suspense, like swinging and missing at the first two pitches. The ball sailed high over the fence as the left fielder helplessly looked up and threw his glove skyward. A home run for a dramatic 13-12 victory! Cheering wildly, the entire Utcaa team escorted me around the bases, while the Ers stood in silence, stunned by their sudden loss.

I could have walked on air that day, but instead I slowly rode home with the gang on our green bicycles, savoring the end of summer. It doesn't get any better than that.

The mystery may be the most popular genre in all fiction. We want the mystery to come to a neat, tidy conclusion by the end of the story, but sometimes the issue is one that is unsolvable.--erw

Nancie W.

When I came to Indiana to visit friends and relatives, some of whom I hadn't seen this century, the last thing I expected to get involved in was a decades old murder case.

"My P.I. license isn't even good in Indiana, Louie."

The rosy-nosed, chubby, and nearly bald man sitting across from me wiped the foam off his lips with the back of his arm and waved off my concern.

"Don't worry, you'll just be one of my sources of information."

My entire face must have scrunched up in confusion. "Source of information about what? I haven't even been around here in years."

"It's a cold case, someone you knew in high school."

"No shit? Why are you on a cold case, Louie?"

"I'm close to retirement, and I don't want any new things comin' up that I can't finish. But cold cases, well, these seldom get solved anyway so it gives me somethin' to do these last few weeks, and we check off that we looked at the file, put it away for a few more years, and there you go. After a case gets this old nobody expects any miracles."

He still hadn't told me who the case involved, just that it was somebody I knew. I hadn't see Louie Nowitzki in years and years. It shocked me to see him on the police force, though I had heard that he had turned over a new leaf sometime after his arrest for car theft back when we were in high school.

It's amazing how many old memories are stored away amidst the dust and tzchotchkes of our minds. Even though I hadn't seen Louie in over thirty years, and hadn't ever given much thought to what had happened to him, sitting here easily brought back the days when we were in school together. Especially the 6th grade, when we punched it out in the alley in back of St. Al's school. I gave him a shiner and a bloody lip that I still felt good about. After that he never bothered me, though he stilled tended to bully the smaller and weaker kids. I'd also heard he'd been disciplined a time or two for roughing up suspects, and once had been suspended. It appeared that he'd survived long enough to be a whisker away from his pension. That's probably the real reason he was on cold cases. Just stay out of trouble Louie, get your pension and go.

The redness in his eyes and the veins in his nose told me that he hadn't conquered all his demons, and if he didn't have something to occupy his time after retirement he could easily become a barfly.

After St. Al's we went to different high schools; the dividing line ran between our houses so I didn't see too much of Louie then, except at a basketball or football game. I'd hear about him around town, nearly always because of something he'd done that bent, teased, or broke the law, but generally not something too serious, other than the car theft.

He stumbled through school needing a few extra classes to get his diploma the summer after the rest of us graduated, and was required to check with the local police station every week to report on his activities. Somehow something clicked, I don't know what it was but more power to him, and Louie joined the Army, became, can you believe it, an MP, then returned to our little home town and joined the police force, eventually becoming a top notch detective. After high school I went to college and then moved to California (after a stint in the Army) and our paths never crossed until this weekend, when the rival high schools were celebrating forty plus years since graduation with a joint reunion.

"Let's get some lunch," Louie suggested. "Been to Arnie's lately?"

"Not in a while; it's still there, eh?"

"Or we could go to the Porcelain Room, if you want sliders?"

Amazing, but there are some things that don't change. Arnie's was a dog house—hot dogs and Polish sausage, with fries. I'd eaten my first dog at Arnie's over fifty years ago and could not guess how many I'd consumed from this shack during the next several years. After school, after a game, for lunch, after work, during work; if we didn't eat here, we ate at White Castle, the home of the slider, those unique hamburgers with the taste that you either loved or hated, no in between.

Amongst all the changes around me--new stores that replaced I can't remember what-- but I knew they hadn't been there when I last visited, Arnie's was the same. In fact, it still had a large parking lot; land that I would have thought had long ago been sold to some builder. Inside it was all familiar, as if I'd been there yesterday. There were a dozen swivel chairs and a menu that was the same as it'd been forever. No ice cream, no cookies, not even coffee. Just dogs, Polish, fries, and a soda, take it or leave it.

There was one little table outside and we took that, the better to talk. I bit into the Polish with gusto, the only way. In between bites I urged Louie to fill me in.

"Let me finish this," I think he said; it was hard to understand him talking with his mouth full. When he had gobbled down both of his dogs he almost made me choke when he said, "You remember Nancie W.?"

I stared at Louie, in mid-bite, my brain scrambling to process the name he had given me and trying to compute whether I had really heard what he'd said. The beautiful girl with the last name that even we Polaks couldn't pronounce. If she'd lived long enough Nancie W. would never have collected Social Security because nobody would have been able to spell her name the same way twice.

I swallowed, washed down with soda, and nodded several times before answering.

"Sure I do." Sure I did, quite well, I should have said, but what business of Louie's was it how well I'd known her?

"I heard she committed suicide several years ago," I said. I had been stunned by that news. Not that I had seen her since I moved to California and not that I had even been asking about her.

"I went to one of the reunions and there were pictures of people from our class who had died. I was really surprised to see her picture. Somebody—I don't remember who—told me they'd heard she taken pills."

Louis nodded vigorously while wiping mustard off his lip with a paper napkin. "Yeah, that was the story. Well, anyway, the way it reads in the file. I heard about it, remembered her slightly, but was never involved. For awhile it was investigated as a possible homicide, but they decided it was an overdose, and there was no indication of foul play."

"And this was when exactly, Louie? What year?"

"1988, July 4th, in fact. Funny way to celebrate the Fourth."

I shut out the here and now and thought back to 1988. What was I doing on the Fourth of July, 1988? Probably went to the local parade, cooked some burgers, watched fireworks in the evening. We used to go to some friends who lived overlooking the Rose Bowl. We'd eat on the deck and watch the show for free. And Nancie was going to sleep and I didn't know it. Well, so what; lots of people die and I don't know it.

'Waddya thinkin', Trixie?" Stunned again, I could only laugh. "Oh man, I haven't heard that name in awhile! You were the only one who called me that, Louie."

He laughed too, almost as if he'd forgotten his nickname for me but had just spit it out from old habits. "Hell, I could never pronounce your name correctly; it's almost as bad as Nancie's. Okay, I'll use Chris for a change."

"Speaking of which, how did you know her?"

"Oh, friends of friends. Never really knew her, just met her a couple of times at a party or picnic or somethin'. Broody, if I recall, never said much, never smiled much."

"Oh? Did you see her senior class picture? That's a smile I remember."

He nodded, probably thinking back to pictures he'd seen in the case file. "Yeah, but those are posed. In real life, at least the couple times I met her, she never seemed to smile."

Why was it that the one thing I remember so precisely about Nancie was her smile and her laugh? Didn't anybody else see her lovely smile, hear her infectious laugh? Were we always alone when she was happy?

"You're thinkin' again," said Louie. "Anything you remember, like somebody who didn't like her or might have wanted to hurt her?"

"No, Louie. You're right, she was moody. I don't think she had a lot of friends. I don't think she ever went to the sports events, or the dances. Too bad. But I can't imagine anybody who'd want to hurt her." I knew she didn't care to go to the sports events, because I invited her several times.

She'd always ask me about the game later, when I would meet her. "We lost," I usually said, because usually we *had* lost. "Close though; better free throw shooting and we might have taken it. What have you been doing?"

"Reading, studying. Let's go get a coke and some fries." So we'd get some food and drive to the lake and park and maybe neck. And we'd talk and laugh and she would smile and say she'd see me in school next week.

And I always would see her, because we had the same homeroom to start the day. But sometimes she'd leave quickly for her classes and I wouldn't see her again all week. Moody, yes.

"So tell me again, Louie, why are you interested in this? Just to fill your time until retirement?"

He shrugged and took time to light a cigarette, sucking on it and expelling a long thread of gray smoke before he spoke again. He was one of the few people I knew anymore that smoked, and really, did I know him anymore?

"Partially, but give me some credit for doing my job pretty well."

I nodded in acceptance of someone else's expertise. I assume he had done his job well enough, screw-off that he was when I knew him when we were growing up.

"Back when the case should have been closed it stayed open, technically, due to some administrative error. So a few years later some dick name of Shannon—an Irish bloke, don't ya know—he takes a look at it and is miffed by some things."

"Such as?"

Louie waved a hand in the air, indicating just 'things'. "No note, no medicine bottle...plus she'd just had a book of poems published. How's about that?"

Yes, I had a copy, sent to me out of the blue when I hadn't even thought of her in years. It was a package postmarked from San Francisco, from the Bay Area Publishing Group. I opened it thinking it was something I had ordered and forgotten about. The book was entitled, 'The Bitter and The Sweet'. The cover showed a woman standing on a beach looking out over the water. The sky was gray all the way to the horizon where it met the equally gray water. To the far right were the rotting remains of a pier. I recognized the place immediately. In the foreground was a bright yellow flower. The author's name was given as Nancie Williams but I knew that the publisher had insisted to the author that if they expected to sell any books she needed to use a name that people could pronounce and spell.

When I opened the book it fell to where a business card was placed, pages 38 and 39. It had Nancie's name on it, her real name, and indicated that she was working in Chicago. On the back of the card was a handwritten note.

'Chris: remember those fireworks we made on our special 4th of July?
I can never forget. I hope your life has been happy and that you are well.
Love forever, Nancie'

I wrote her a letter to the address on her business card. A few weeks later I got a note back from a vice-president telling me she had passed away unexpectedly. I was stunned beyond words but somehow I couldn't--or wouldn't--grieve for her. I no longer knew anyone who had known her so I buried my sadness deep in a musty corner of my mind and went on. A few years later I was at a reunion and someone—I no longer remember who—told me she had committed suicide. I wanted to cry but couldn't. I couldn't grasp that someone I had known could do such a thing. Again, I couldn't grieve.

"When I went through the file I also noticed there had been an error made with the fingerprints."

I waited for Louie to go on. He waited for me to ask a question. I out waited him.

"Right from the start it looked like a suicide. No wounds on the...on her, no weapons around, no sign of a struggle. But no pill bottle was found or any evidence of medicine that she might have overdosed on. No drugs, no signs that she'd ever taken any. So they proceeded to process the site as if it was a homicide, but when the coroner confirmed she had enough sleeping pills in her to doze off into eternity, that was that."

"And the prints?"

"They were sent off, and nothing came of them. The only prints they found were hers, those from an eighty-year old lady who lived next door, and one that was ID'd as a stepbrother."

"Oh? I didn't know she had a stepbrother."

"Yeah, well, the old lady next door confirmed that there was a guy who visited occasionally and Nancie said he was her stepbrother from Wisconsin. The file shows that it was confirmed he'd been to see her a week before she died, and prior to that date three or four times in the past couple years. He didn't know anything about her using pills, nothing about a boy friend, enemies, nothing much."

"She never married?" I asked. I knew she hadn't.

"Guess not. Strange, uh? I mean even if she was moody she was one good looker, wasn't she."

I looked Louie in the eyes and said yeah, she was, trying not to sound too agreeable.

She sure was, especially when she did smile. First time I saw her was when she dropped a book on my foot. (It was our junior year and later I wondered why I hadn't met her sooner.) When I fumbled the book trying to pick it up she thought that was funny and for a second I thought she had dropped it on purpose, just to get a reaction. Thinking back now, I wonder if she did. She stifled a laugh and soon we discovered that we both had a study hall period in the library in a few minutes so we walked together. We spent the next hour whispering in the library and by the time the bell rang I felt I had known her for years. Yet, two years later she didn't show up at the graduation ceremonies and no one seemed to miss her except me. Louis was speaking and I forced myself to listen up.

"According to the file there were prints on her high school year book, the one from her senior year. Your senior year, too, Chris."

"I still have that one too, somewhere in the garage." When I'd decided to come back for this year's reunion I dug out my senior class yearbook from a box of old photos, playbills and letters. We all looked bright-eyed and eager in perfectly posed sittings, just like thousands of year books at thousand of high schools across the country. There were lots of handsome and pretty faces; didn't we all look great? Young and eager and promising. Nancie wasn't the most beautiful girl in our class, but she was as attractive as any.

I had been eager to see what elegant and loving words she would write in my book. Of course since she wasn't at graduation it was late when I finally got her to sign my book. Instead of eloquence she chose humor, to make fun of me, I felt.

> 'High school is over
> And you've been a peach
> I loved the nights
> We parked at the beach
> Burma Shave'

Now, I treasured it because it was fun; not as serious as most of her writing was.

"But when I looked at the file—and when we work a cold case like this the new guy, me in this instance, tries to forget the conclusion of whoever else looked at it, and looks at everything as if it's the first time."

I nodded knowingly; I'm not a dummy, Louie. He stamped out his cigarette in the paper plate that held the remains of his French fries, coughed lightly, and folded his hands together and looked at me as if he might finally be getting to the point.

"They weren't the prints of the brother."

Aha! Aha, what? So, is this were we go to commercial and the audience is held spellbound. What the hell was he getting at? Okay, I gave in and asked him.

"Who's were they Louie?"

"Well, we don't know yet," he said, as if I was a dummy for not figuring that out.

"They are somewhat deteriorated but I sent them out again. But an old case like this, it takes awhile to get to the head of the class."

"You sent in the old print card?" Yes, he nodded.

"And so where is the year book itself?"

"Probably back at the house."

Getting more confused, I asked. "What house? For God's sake Louie, don't make me have to pull this out of you!"

"The same house she lived in when she was in high school; the same house she lived in when she died. You must know it. Weren't you ever there?"

"She was still living there?" Yeah, her house, the one that was usually dark except for a light in her bedroom where she always seemed to be if she was home. The house where we first *did it*. At least, where I first did it; she said it was the first time for her too, but I didn't believe that then and don't believe it now, but I never cared if she was telling the truth or not.

She lived there with her parents, an only child, I thought. Never a mention about a stepbrother or any other relatives. Oh yeah, a crazy old grandfather in a rest home north of Chicago, but that's all. I rarely met her parents; it was like she was ashamed of them, or maybe ashamed of me. It was a nice house; not fancy, but well-maintained and clean, at least the parts of it I saw. I stopped by once after I'd been working at the store one Sunday afternoon and she came out on the porch to greet me. I saw her Mom in the background and Nancie was forced to introduce me. She seemed nice enough, and pretty, too, like a grown-up Nancie.

"You shouldn't come by without calling," she said. "My parents think I'm too young to have a boyfriend."

I was surprised to learn I was her 'boyfriend', but liked it. After that, she would often invite me over when her parents were away. "We have a cottage at Bass Lake. We go there every summer, all the holidays, all the time except in the winter when it gets too cold there. I'm tired of it and now that I'm in high school they don't force me to go. I always have homework and studying to do so they let me stay home. They meet the Kaminskis so it's more fun for them without me around anyway."

So many the Friday or Saturday evening or Sunday afternoon I spent there with her. Except she insisted I go to the basketball or football games because she knew I enjoyed them. "I won't let you in until I know the game is over. You shouldn't spend all your time with me."

The first few times all we did was talk and study—really, we did, and listen to records or watch television. Eventually I wanted to do more. She always deflected my clumsy advances by reaching for her book of poetry. "You have to love me for my mind, first, sweetie," she would say, and laugh a laugh so sweet I couldn't resist but join in the laughter and would sit back nicely to listen to her.

'So when the life I have
Meets the one I wish for
Why go on anymore?'

I wasn't sure what that meant; I thought she might explain it to me but if she did I wasn't paying attention. It was getting dark, it was cozy sitting on her bed, and I wanted to touch her tits, not her mind. Eventually...well, no need to think about that old memory.

"A few times," I finally answered Louie's question. "I'm surprised she was still there. What about her parents; gone?"

Louie nodded, then interrupted the atmosphere by suggesting what we needed was a cold beer. "You been to the Sportmans' Club lately?" he asked.

"Louie, I haven't been in the Region in years. But I guess I shouldn't be surprised it's still there." Like I say, you go back home and so much has changed that it's almost a shock, but it's nice when you find the things that haven't changed. Bars come and go but the Sportman's has been there since the invention of beer, we used to say.

I almost expected to see Pixie in there, his home away from home, but then recalled he had passed away a year ago or so, the victim, likely, of too many beers and sausages. We grabbed a booth in the rear, near the pool tables, and ordered a couple of drafts. Louie continued as if we hadn't had a fifteen minute interruption in our conversation.

"The way I hear it, she went to Northwestern after graduation from Elsie. But after a year her Dad died, cancer or heart, I don't know, so she's back and forth to spend time with her mother. I got some of this from old Tubby Kowalski; you remember him?"

"Oh, yeah, is he still around? Bet he weighs 300 by now."

Louie nodded but didn't laugh; after all, he was probably on the north side of 225 pounds himself.

"Then about the time Nancie finishes college her Mom gets real sick, so Nancie moves back home to care for her. When she died, Nancie inherited the house. I guess the stepbrother got stiffed, but I don't really know about that. So again she comes back for awhile and lives there until she can get through doing what you have to do when your parents are gone. Probably tough if you're alone." A rare morsel of compassion coming from Louie, I noted. But then he was an only child, I recalled, so maybe he's been there.

"She kept the house for herself and moved in after she finished college. Then she taught school for awhile; guess where?"

I knew the answer but shrugged ignorance. Louie waited so I guessed, "L.C."

"That's right, for two years."

I could never get my mother to see the humor in the way the kids from the other schools 'mooed' us at our games.

"Mom, you know it's Lewis and Clark High School..."

"I know that, son, I went to school there."

"Okay, so Lewis & Clark is shortened to L.C...."

"I know that too. We called it L.C. for short when I was there. But what's with the moos?"

"Well, L.C. becomes Elsie; you now, the cow—so the kids from the other schools, they moo us."

She shook her head. "I still don't get it. It's not funny."

Whatever.

"After that she took a job in Chi with some psychological consulting firm. I don't understand what she did there, but she was still working for them when...when she died."

That would have been the Midwest Employee Advisory Group, I knew, from the business card she had sent me with the book of poems. She was so smart, but she took these jobs that didn't pay much. I guess she got some satisfaction out of it. I wondered if any of my letters to her survived. Was Louis going to dump this on me, or had Nancie destroyed our correspondence?

Not that there was much to our correspondence. A letter a year, at best. After I moved to California I had no idea where she was. It didn't dawn on me that she was still in the same house until I got a letter from her. She gushed about her work, but between the lines something was missing.

I wrote her back, asking if she was married or had a boyfriend. She never responded to that. In fact, she didn't respond for years. I didn't want to push it; it's not like I was pining for her or anything. After all, she was the one who always made it difficult.

She hadn't show up for the graduation ceremonies. I looked all over for her. Then I ran all over town to every party I knew of looking for her. No one had seen her. Most people I asked didn't know who I was talking about. I went to her house and found it totally dark. Still, I knocked on the door for five minutes; threw pebbles on her bedroom window. No one answered.

For weeks I called nearly every day. If anyone answered it was her mother and she always said Nancie wasn't home. She said she was working and she would take a message. When I asked where she was working her Mom told me Nancie couldn't be disturbed at work and would hang up.

It was July 3rd when I saw her again. She was waiting for me when I got out of work at 11:30 at night.

"Where have you been?" I asked, trying not to act as pissed as I felt.

"Oh, visiting friends, working, doing things with my folks. Getting ready for college, too, you know. Aren't you going?"

"You know I am. We talked about that a thousand times, Nancie. You still going to Northwestern?"

"Yes, but never mind that. Are you free now?"

I was supposed to be back at work early in the morning and was going to spend the night with some of the guys playing cards. My folks didn't expect me home.

"I'm yours, sweetheart," I said, in my best Bogart imitation.

I followed her in my car to her house. We went straight to her bedroom where a bottle of iced champagne in a bucket awaited us.

"To celebrate our graduation," she said, beaming that smile at me that nearly melted the ice and sent shivers tickling my groin.

"It's about time. Christ, Nancie, I've been looking for you ever since graduation. Where were you?"

"Shh." She touched my lips with a finger and then kissed me; just enough to tease me. Then she poured champagne.

"I've never had champagne," I admitted. "Have you?"

She nodded. "Sometimes at our cottage, when my folks are partying. Let's sit down."

We sat on her bed and sipped the bubbly. She put music on; soft stuff—I don't remember the name but once in awhile even now the tune comes back to me when I least expect it but I still can't recall the name. Maybe I don't want to know the name.

After awhile we leaned back and cuddled. I was so horny I thought I would explode. She kissed me firmly, then aggressively, like never before. It would be years before anyone kissed me like that again. Then she turned away and I thought I heard a sob.

"What's wrong? Are you crying?"

"Yes. No. Oh, never mind, you idiot. Just hold me and don't talk."

As an adult I certainly learned that men can never expect to understand women. As a teenager what could you expect from me? But even then I wondered if Nancie had some...issue, I called it, not wanting to think, 'problem' , that made her so melancholy. Now I like melancholy, to an extent. I think it's an important mood in human experience, but at 18 years of age, I was over my head. All I knew was that I held a lovely girl in my arms, a sobbing one who wanted me to hold her, and so I did.

I lay there at least a couple hours after she fell asleep, listening to the radio and occasionally kissing her on the forehead. Eventually I nodded off.

When I awoke it was to the most beautiful crystal blue eyes I could ever hope to see or imagine. Nancie wore a smile that could have melted Iceland, and nothing else. I'd never seen her like this before. The other times I'd been with her it had been groping clumsily in the shadows in the car at the beach, or under the covers. My God she was beautiful. It was as if light itself emanated from her skin. I just lay there and luxuriated.

I saw her again the next weekend but then she had to go to Evanston to get ready for college. I was going to a local school and I too got caught up in full time college, a part time job, Pixie's softball team, and in no time at all it was Christmas.

Nancie called me on Christmas Eve and I dashed over to her house after Midnight Mass. I didn't even ask why her parents were gone and she was home alone on Christmas. I'd bought her a pendant that I thought was pretty fancy; it cost more money than I had ever spent on a gift for a girl—in fact, it was probably the first time I'd ever bought a gift for someone I thought of as a 'girlfriend'.

I hated to leave her that night but figured I better sneak back home before Christmas morning dawned. And so it would go for the next couple of years—a stolen few hours when she was home to care for her mother, and sometimes, glory be, she'd invite me to Evanston for a long weekend. We even went to football games and I sensed that the melancholy that seemed to be her prevailing mood was being eased out. Maybe school away from home was good for her.

We were both too busy to make commitments. The days passed freakishly fast. Before I could turn around I had graduated, started a job but barely got going before Uncle Sam came calling. I couldn't get a hold of Nancie and it wasn't till I was in 'Nam that I heard from her. Somehow she'd gotten my address. She was teaching at Lewis & Clark, I was glad to hear, but I was disappointed that her words lacked the affection she had shown me up to the last rendezvous we shared.

"So it was just a coincidence that you were in town this week just when I'm working the case."

Louie was speaking; I wasn't sure how long I'd been preoccupied with my thoughts. He'd been watching a game on TV so maybe I hadn't missed much of what he said.

"Coincidence? Louie, I thought homicide dicks didn't believe in coincidence."

He chuckled wickedly while lighting a cigarette, coughing as he still laughed while trying to inhale.

"Tell ya the truth, Chris. But first, you tell me; you were nailin' her weren't you?"

"Let's not go there, Louie."

"Why not? It's ancient history, for God's sake. You can tell me."

"I wouldn't be a gentleman then, would I?"

"Yeah, bull. But Okay, keep it to yourself. But about six months ago I ran in to old Tubby, like I told you. Somehow the talk came to old times and who was where and what so-and-so was doing, and the next thing is he's telling me how when he worked at the Castle he used to see you and ole Nancie W. all the time. Said you guys were two of his best customers."

I nodded. No need to deny that. "Yeah, we loved sliders, but her especially. And so from that you decided I might have an idea of what happened to her twenty-five years later?"

"Eh, you know us nosy cops. Leave no stone unturned. I didn't know how to find you right off, and it didn't seem like a big deal until I looked into the case."

I knew he wasn't finished as he puffed away and stared up at the television. He pointed at me and said, "Did ya ever get the notion that Tubby had a thing for Nancie? You know, maybe he was hot for her."

I hadn't ever thought of it. Now I tried to remember and it seemed, though maybe I was forcing a memory, that he did use to leer at her. "Can't say for sure. I always thought he was kind of sleazy in any case, Louie. Why, what are you getting at?"

"Let's go," he said abruptly and rose up, his belly straining to squeeze out of the booth.

"Now where, Hot Dog John's maybe?"

"Nah, that's long gone, Trix. No, let's go over to the house."

"*The* house?"

"Yeah, I'll drive and bring you back here."

On the way over Louie explained that after Nancie died the house went to her stepbrother, who came down from Wisconsin to handle things. He rented the house for lack of knowing what to do with it. Shortly after the renter skipped out it was rented again on long term lease to one Joseph H. Kowalksi."

It took me just a second or two. "Joseph H. You mean Tubby?"

He nooded as he made a right turn onto the street where Nancie used to live. "The house is vacant again though and the stepbrother has it up for sale now. I got him to let the realtor give me the key, for police business. He wasn't happy, like what the hell do the police want with an old suicide case."

"What'd you do, slap him around?"

"Ha, that's good, Chris! Nah, he said okay, long as I didn't interfere with any potential buyers."

The house looked smaller than I remembered and a little run-down. It needed painting. "So is no one living here now? What happened to Tubby?"

Louie didn't exactly answer my question but he said, "Not here any more. I told you it was up for sale."

We went in and at first nothing seemed familiar. But then I recalled that I never paid any attention to most of the house. We always went straight to Nancie's room and that's where we spent our time, other that an occasional foray to the kitchen.

But her room looked frighteningly familiar. The furniture looked the same; the book shelves, the drapes, even the color of the walls. This was the room where I had spent so many happy hours. Hours with Nancie, talking and laughing, studying, listening to records, sitting on her bed while she read me her poetry, cuddling and smooching, falling asleep in her arms, or vice versa, waking up at the quiet, meditative hour of three a.m. to find myself next to her. Those were some times, yes indeed.

"You were here a few times, right," said Louie, a statement, not a question.

I nodded. "The brother rented it with furniture and all, didn't he?"

This time Louie nodded.

"It smells musty, or stale," said Louie.

It didn't have her scent anymore, that was why.

Louie reached to the shelf and pulled off a book, so smoothly it was if he planed his exact move for when we entered this room.

"Her senior year book." He handed it to me.

"Where you found the prints you couldn't identify?"

"They were Tubby's," he said.

"I thought you said they…"

"I wasn't ready to tell you."

"But if all this was here while he rented the house, then so what if you found his prints?"

"You idiot! What kind of detectives they got there in the land of sunshine? His prints were found on the book back in '88, right after she died. What were they doing on this book then? I don't think Tubby and Nancie were close friends, do you?"

I felt incredibly stupid. "No, definitely not," I said after several seconds.

I opened the book to the back where blank pages had been left for people to sign and leave their witty remarks for posterity. I had thought for weeks about what I would write in her book. Something for the ages, something we would both treasure no matter what happened to us in the decades to come. I found it and read my words. I knew Louie had already read them.

"Dumb," I said.

"Eh, not bad for a kid," Louie said. He was right.

Like a magician Louie then produced another book. It was a copy of 'The Bitter and The Sweet'. By habit I opened it to page 39, and then quickly closed it. "This is the book you said she had written just before she died?"

Louie looked at me, not believing I didn't know of the book. "Yeah," he mumbled.

I was getting angry; at Louie, at Nancie, at myself.

"So what in the good name of God are we doing here, Louie? What's the purpose?"

He hesitated, as if marshalling his thoughts, but I could tell he was deciding whether to answer my question or forget the whole thing.

"I told you I saw old Tubby a few months ago, and we got to talking."

"Yeah, yeah, he said he saw us at White Castle. So what?"

"You know, I never liked the guy, but we got talking about old days, what happened to who, all that crap, and we were near Sportsman's so we went over for a beer. Now I'm telling you I never socialized with the guy, but it was kind of fun and we got a little tipsy, laughing and all.

"He kept comin' back to you and Nancie. Said he followed you guys a few times from the Castle."

I perked up.

"Over to the beach. He watched you guys."

"What? Are you serious? That bastard watched Nancie and me?"

Louie nodded. "A time or two, he said."

I sighed, a corny expression, but that's what I did. "Lot of the times all we did was talk."

"Hmm. That would have disappointed him, I think."

I shot him a glare.

"Anyway, I wasn't too drunk and it got me to thinkin' that he was obsessed with Nancie. I mean, it's been a long time, ya know."

"Tell me about it," I said, the bitterness seeping out. I wanted to hit something and Tubby sounded like the target that would do best.

"Then he told me he'd been living in her house; rented it from her step-brother. I began to get the chills. It sounded ghoulish somehow, coming from him, ya know, after tellin' me he used to spy on you two."

I was getting angrier and impatient. "So what are you leading to, Louie? You think he killed her?"

He shrugged, put his hand out in a gesture of uncertainty. "It's possible. You know, he wasn't a complete dummy. He took a couple years at the local campus, got himself a job with some pharmaceutical supply house over on the south side."

Again I perked up.

"He could have gotten pills for her."

"I don't see how she could have ever had any contact with him, Louie."

"He might have been persistent, maybe he followed her, ya know, like he did when she and you went to the beach. He might have made a pass at her and she put him off. So he decided to kill her out of spite."

"But you said there was no sign of violence at the...here." God, but it hit me suddenly...here, where we had loved each other, she had died. I became dizzy. "Let's get out of here, Louie; I need fresh air."

He understood and followed me out onto the front porch where we sat down on the top step.

"He might have assisted her," Louie suggested.

"Louie, she was a smart girl. She could have gotten pills on her own, if she wanted. She could have gotten pills to ease her depression, too, if she wanted to. Even back then they had stuff."

"He was a big guy, Chris. He might have forced the pills down and not even have left a sign. It's possible."

"So are you going to arrest him?" Louie said nothing and didn't look at me.

"Wait a minute; you said 'was a big guy'. What happened, Louie?"

"Tubby died in a car accident, just a few weeks after I talked to him."

"Was he drinking?" I asked.

Louie shook his head. "Maybe a little, but mostly he was just unlucky. One of those things. So then a few months later I get told to wind down by looking over some of these cases and I come across this one. It got me thinkin', that's all."

"But you've got no case, Louie."

"I know, I know."

"No, really, you've got no case against Tubby. Nancie would never have let him get close enough to her, physically or emotionally. She must have accumulated the pills over time, to use when she felt she needed to."

"And the prints?"

"Damn if I know; maybe he looked her up after graduation. Hey, did he write anything in her book?"

"Yeah, somethin' really silly. I don't remember exactly. You want to read it?"

"No, but I'm sure I would have noticed if he'd signed her book before I did, and I didn't until a couple of weeks after graduation. Maybe he even broke in here if he was so obsessed with her."

"Yeah, I kinda been thinkin' the same thing. But why did she do it then? I mean, she had a good job, probably still a nice lookin' gal, and she just got her book published...I don't get it."

"I have no answer to that Louie. I knew her, she was odd at times, but all teenagers seem odd if you stop to think about it."

We were silent then for awhile. I don't know what Louie was thinking but I was once more wondering if there had ever been an indication that I should have noticed. But I'd been through that a number of times with myself.

Answering myself, I said aloud, "Hell, Louie, I never once thought she might be suicidal. What were you doing at eighteen, Louie, other than trying to get laid or get high?"

"I just thought... when I heard a reunion was comin' up I called Jean. She said yeah, you were comin'. So I thought...maybe I was wrong...I thought you might be interested. Maybe have some perspective. Sorry if I did wrong."

I reached over and squeezed his substantial shoulder. It was about as close as he and I would get to expressing fondness. "You did the right thing, Louie. Thanks."

We drove back in silence to where I'd left my car. Louie parked and we sat there for a moment. He spoke first.

"So what kind of cases ya got back there, buddy?"

"Cases? Oh, hell, Louis I'm no more a private detective than you are a brain surgeon!"

"What? But I read..."

"Louie, I was a marketing rep for several firms in Southern California. I made a good living and now I'm retired. When the reunion came up and they asked people for a short bio, I thought it'd be a kick to put some stuff in there just for laughs. So I said I'd become a P.I. to see if anybody reads those things."

"You asshole!" he said as he bashed me in the arm.

"Oh! Hey, that hurt!"

"Yeah? As much as when I hit you with that pitch back in Little League?"

"That's right, you got me good that time."

"Yeah, well, that's for what you did in the alley, so I think we're even."

Again we fell silent for a moment. I eased the door open and said, "Have a good retirement, Louie."

"Yeah, you too, pal."

As I sat in the plane waiting for take off I felt like a weight was descending on me. But I shook it off and once we were airborne I ordered a scotch and soda. When we reached cruising altitude I looked down on the fluffy clouds and thought it would be wonderful if the plane could land on them and the passengers could jump out and romp in the sky. The sun was bright and it was a beautiful day. But my thoughts came back to Nancie's book.

I had read it eagerly shortly after receiving it, happy to believe that she was doing well. Many of the poems I knew, Nancie having read them to me. Yes, there was still an overall tone of sadness, but I figured that if she bothered to get them organized and published, then she was okay and things were working out for her.

They were mostly long poems that could stand alone but as a whole made up a passage in the lifetimes of several people; people that Nancie had either imagined or known. The exception was one very short section that initially I didn't pay any attention to. After I learned how she had died I read the book again, and when I came to page 39 I read several times the words that now blazed at me and made me feel shallow for not having noticed them on my first reading.

'It was only you
Who wanted my smile
Only you who loved my laugh
My silliness, my moods
But I knew we'd part
My sadness couldn't cope
But love you, I still do
More now that I'm gone'

When I get home, I promised, I will take a long walk in the woods and maybe scream at the sky or kick a pine cone or two. I tipped my glass and silently toasted: to the bitter, and to the sweet.

This is just a reminder not to take things too seriously. Most of the things we keep track of today will be meaningless once we are gone...like our golf scores!--erw

Pegging

"It's been a fun evening, Charlie, thanks for the games."

"Fun? Are you sure, Joe? It was fun for me, but then I won eight of the ten games."

Joe shrugged, his wrinkles gyrating across his face and his mouth squinching his gray mustache up against his nose as he started to speak, changed his mind, then changed it again.

"Ahh, Charlie, I enjoy playing cribbage even when I lose. I didn't use to, but for a long time now I've just enjoyed playing, and if I lose to you, well, you were due to win a few."

"A few, hey! Lately I've been putting it to you pretty good, old-timer. I've gained about a thousand points in the past few weeks. Which, you know, means a thousand dollars."

"What, you're keeping score now? I thought that was my job?" asked Joe, as he bent his arms into the sleeves of the brown cardigan.

"Yeah, I know, but when was the last time you summarized the score? It's been years. At least, it's been years since you told me the score. Maybe I'm edging ahead, hey Joe?" Charlie nodded several times quickly.

"C'mon, Charlie, who cares anymore? We're over seventy years old and I really don't think it matters who owes whom a few dollars. We quit worrying about that back when we still played for penny a point. I've got the scores entered, sure, I do that after every time we play. But honestly, Charlie, I haven't totaled the scores in at least ten years."

Joe put his hand on the doorknob and turned to go. Then he turned back to look at his friend. "But hell's bells, Charlie, you know I'm a better player than you!"

Joe laughed his deep, gruff chortle that had been such a pleasing sound to Joe's wife of forty years, years that had ended with her passing two years ago. But from Charlie it was worth a soft punch in the arm.

"Play tomorrow, Joe?"

"No, make it Friday. Molly and her kids are visiting tomorrow. Come to my place, OK?"

"Sure, but listen Joe, seriously now. I've been thinking, and I know you've won more games than I have, but I have had a great streak of luck lately. So I've been wondering what the overall score is after all these years. It might be fun to total 'em up and see."

Joe reached into his pocket and pulled out the piece of paper on which he'd written the results of this evening's games. He looked at them for a moment as if he already forgotten what they were.

"I don't know, Charlie. Like I said, I always record the scores, but it's mostly habit. I've always been that way, keeping records of everything. But for what reason I'm not sure. I'd just as soon quit keeping score and throw all those records away. You know they go back over twenty years?"

Charlie nodded his head several times, slower this time. "Remember when we started to keep score, penny a point, dime a game? Then we raised the ante a little at a time, until now it's 25 points a game and a dollar a point. Maybe that means we've been successful, eh Joe? Why don't you total up those points and find out who owes who how much? I mean, here I've won maybe $1000 in the past few games and haven't seen the color of your money yet!"

They both laughed as they recalled how, years, even decades ago, they had started to play cribbage, very casually at first, and then, as happens with competitive people who take their card games seriously, began to keep close score while playing for money. Except that they never paid each other off; since the fun of it was that they were involved in an ongoing, indefinite tournament, no payoff need be made until the tournament was over. And they knew it would never end, until one of them was gone. But after each session Joe would enter the scores on his note pad, and then transcribe into an official-looking book the scores of the games, the winner, skunks, even the date. Charlie didn't want to do this chore but he encouraged Joe to.

"Maybe now you owe me a couple thousand, Joe. I could use that for a nice vacation."

Charlie, the shorter of the two men peeked his eyes upward from under the thick, fluffy eyebrows at his friend Joe, who still stood with his hand on the doorknob. There was a smile on Charlie's face but Joe knew the look; when that look came over Charlie it meant he was serious, as he usually was about money.

"No way, Charlie, I'm sure I'm still ahead, so I won't add 'em up. Who cares now, anyway? We've both got enough money to last us, so why bother." He waved away the idea with a grunt and another tug at the door, but he knew Charlie wasn't ready to drop the subject yet. I should leave, Joe thought. I know I've beaten Charlie through the years, but I'm afraid if I show him it might hurt his feelings. Yet, this recent hot streak of Charlie's had lasted quite awhile now. It seems over the last month Charlie had won about 80 per cent of the games, an unusually extended wining streak. Maybe that has evened things up and now Charlie wants to find out. He's never suggested we do this before; it's been an unspoken rule that we would never end the tournament; it would just die when one of us did. Am I afraid to find out? What if he is ahead, would that bother me?

Joe looked at his friend and raised one of his long arms and placed it gently on Charlie's shoulder.

"Charlie, we're both competitive people, or at least we were when we were younger. It meant something to win then, even a card game. So we bet because it was fun to have something at stake, to have something to win or lose. And then we got older, more mature, I hope, a little wealthier, and competition lost its appeal. Not completely, of course. I enjoy beating you at cribbage as much as ever, and..." he removed his arm from Charlie's shoulder and pointed, a jabbing, tender pointing that dear friends can do without irritating the other... "I even enjoy cribbage when I lose, which is what I like to think is mature competition."

A younger person watching and listening to this conversation between two seventy-five year old men might become impatient with their slow, contemplative manner, the pauses between sentences as if the speaker was thinking carefully of what he needed to say in an important diplomatic conference. It wasn't that they were slow thinkers or careful speakers, but that they were both thoughtful men, aware of their pasts, secure in their lives, proud and happy in their memories in these last years of their lives. When they spoke as friends of things that had happened, it reminded them of days long gone but not forgotten. They thought about them and relished the memories, for they knew that tomorrow the memories might fade a little more, and be a little harder to recall.

Joe continued. "Why bring up something we've written off, Charlie? One of us would then be, what, a loser? In games maybe, but we aren't losers, Charlie." The twinkle in Joe's eyes, a large, hard-looking man who had a sensitivity he'd tried to conceal most of his life because it often caused his eyes to water, was just that, a tear or two.

"I agree with all that, Joe, but we did say that some day we'd figure out who owed what and pay off. Of course I know that then we figured some day one of us would move away and the games would end. But here we are, in the same neighborhood all these years. But it might be interesting, or am I being too competitive for you!" Charlie poked Joe as he laughed, trying to make a joke.

Joe didn't laugh, just shrugged. "Well, maybe, I don't know if I'll have time. I've gotta' go now, it's late. Come by Friday, we'll play on my home court for a change. See you."

With that Joe ended the conversation, an odd conversation that gave him a strange, uneasy feeling. He couldn't describe the feeling, the kind that makes you feel something is bothering you but you can't put a finger on what it is, but if you could you'd realize it was something that wasn't really that important. Ah, I must be getting older than I thought, Joe said to himself as he buttoned his sweater and walked down the path to his car.

When he was home Joe went to his library and slumped into his chair, 'the Chair', the well-broken-in lounge chair that had been molded over the years to fit his aging body as if it had been custom built around him. In his hands he held the paper with the scores of the evening's ritual and the bookkeeper's record book in which he had faithfully recorded the results of the cribbage games. Joe had always been a dedicated record keeper. Not just of the ordinary, mundane things like checks, medical expenses, etc. Oh, he kept those too, but his joy was to keep records of trips he had taken, especially those he and Marie had taken together, of ball games he had seen in person, of movies he had seen, books he'd read, and of the 'Ongoing, Unending, First and Only Lifelong Cribbage Tournament Between Joe Jones and Charlie Olsen'.

He opened the book, which was only the latest in a series of ledgers. Each page had the relevant columns titled with the headings Joe had used for decades. There were three double-columns, one for 'Wins', one for 'Points', and one for 'Skunks', with each of their names listed. He unfolded the paper on which he'd recorded that evening's games and officially entered the results. In the 'Wins' column he entered only 2 under his name, 8 under Charlie's. In points he entered the total points for the games: at 25 points for a win that was 200 for Charlie, 50 for himself. Charlie also won one 'Skunk' so Joe entered an additional 25 points. Then, checking his scratch sheet, he entered the total point differential from the games: 30 for himself, having won one game by 19 points and another by 11, and for Charlie he entered 159, the total point spread in his eight wins.

Joe had lied. He had lied to Charlie by his attitude of unconcern about the overall record. Joe knew he was ahead of Charlie in total points, simply because he was a slightly better player. Not enough to give him an appreciable advantage, but enough to gain the edge over an extended series of games, like over twenty-five years or so. But as Joe looked at the ledger and at the scores for the past several series he noticed an unusual repetition of high scores and games won for Charlie. Usually Joe entered the scores without paying much attention to them, though he'd been aware that lately he couldn't seem to buy a simple double-run. A quick mental calculation showed him that in the past two months, which normally represented about twenty series of five or six games, Charlie had gained over 1700 points on Joe. That is a lot of points and could mean the overall score is much closer now than Joe would have estimated.

He idly flipped through the pages, noticing how many times the points for games won was only 25 or even none, because on average one won as often as the other. If asked to guess, Joe would have said they'd won about the same number of games, maybe he a few more, but the point spread would be in Joe's favor because he had skunked Charlie many more times than the reverse. He was reminded of one of tonight's games, when he couldn't get that one point he needed to avoid a skunk. He'd guessed wrong, and only had 90 points when Charlie scored his 121st, and the game ended, the 31 point difference giving Charlie a big gain of 81 points: 25 for the win, 25 bonus for winning by more than 30 (the skunk), and the 31 point differential.

Uncomfortably he thought of the times one or the other would tease about a marked deck, during a particularly good, or bad, streak. In cribbage, though the overall average is for the wins to even out between equal players, it isn't unusual for first one, then the other, to have a streak when he wins several games in a row, or eight of ten, as Charlie had been doing lately. When one got hot, he could do no wrong. You could be holding a 4,5,7,7, and your opponent would cut a 6. When that starts, as the old adage goes, 'good cards will overcome bad playing.' And, of course, 'good playing can be stymied by bad cards.' Now, was that an old adage or not? Seems to me, Joe thought, that I made up that adage myself. Well, if so, it's old by now. Anyway, Charlie wouldn't cheat me, not now, not after all these years. Why would he, when we've gone along for years playing these games, complaining when we couldn't get a good hand, laughing with glee at the rare 'double-skunk', but quickly forgetting the outcome of a game and going on to the next one. Am I really concerned about the bet we'd made all those years ago? I wonder what the score differential is, after all.

I won't think about it tonight, but tomorrow, yes tomorrow I'll get out the old adding machine and spend some time totaling these numbers. I'm tired of keeping score, of keeping ledgers. He looked up from his chair towards the top shelves of the bookcase, up at the dusty ledgers that lay piled there, the ledgers of his personal finances, business finances, list of things he'd done; not exactly a diary as much as a documentary of his life. He'd always found it difficult to open up his personality and deepest thoughts even with pen and paper, so his life history was recorded in cold, precise facts. List: salary, expenses, savings, investments; places visited this year, books read, work done on the house this year-- (not, 'spent the weekend painting the living room a light shade of yellow, the shade that Marie loves so much. She was so happy to see the color appearing on the wall as if by magic as I rolled away, working hard but enjoying it because she enjoyed the result'.) Instead: March 23, 1958; painted living room and bathroom.

It had been his way to keep his life organized and running smoothly, or at least with the appearance of smoothness. After Marie died he'd slacked off in his record keeping. By then he'd retired and sold his machine shop so there were no more business records, and now, when his life consisted of an occasional short trip, visits with his daughter Molly and her family, reading, some odd jobs that he worked on in the garage—a small repair for a neighbor—and the frequent cribbage games with Charlie, the only records he kept any more were of those cribbage games.

He slammed the book shut, and eased himself out of the chair. He looked up at the top shelf again. This weekend, they all go in the trash.

That night Joe dreamt of numbers: a count of 15 for two points; a count of 30 and a 'Go' for a point; double-run for eight points and the Jack for one more. He dreamt that Charlie could see right through Joe's cards and always knew what Joe held. Charlie was pegging points so fast that in one game he pegged out and won, 121 points to Joe's three, on the first hand. The Joe in the dream stared in disbelief. "But that's impossible! It isn't possible to win on the first hand!"

"Well, it was a great hand," said Charlie. "Let's see, 25 points for the win, 118 points for the spread, and what do I get for a triple-skunk, a thousand points?"

"But there is no such thing," Joe protested.

The conjured Joe sat there, hypnotized as Charlie scored his point on the cribbage board. "But that's a google points, Charlie!"

Marie came over and held Joe's hand. That calmed him and when he awoke, he lay there for several minutes re-running the dream, and stopping it when Marie held his hand.

Joe was not a brooder; thinking of Marie did not make him sad. It was a joy to remember the mornings when they awoke simultaneously and smiled a good morning at each other. He popped out of bed refreshed and shortly was hard at work summarizing over twenty years of cribbage games.

The task was tiresome and depressing. It would have been easier if he'd converted the data to a computer spreadsheet, but by the time he'd become computer literate it seemed silly to re-enter all those years of score sheets.

Though Joe appreciated numbers and statistics and the stories they told, something about the totality of these numbers depressed him. Is this all there is to our friendship? Is this all Charlie and I have going? No, that's not true, for they still, now both widowers, enjoyed evenings of conversation and companionship, watching sports, and had other friends they associated with too. They had memories, and true, the cribbage game summary did remind him of the enjoyment the competition had given him. But I don't need these ledgers, just as I don't need a list of Marie's qualities to remind me of her. Or a list of places we visited to remember the fun we had. Sighing, he returned to the task.

It took him several hours. The totals flabbergasted him. Almost 10,000 games of cribbage in 24 years and 9 months! He worked out more statistics: 33.6 games per month on average, but 20 games a week for the last five years. The points were even more fascinating. For the first 24 years and seven months Joe had built a seemingly insurmountable 1,855-point lead. But in the last two months Charlie had worked off nearly 1800 points off the lead that Joe had built up over such a long, long time. After 9,990 games, hours and hours of card playing, of counting points, of pegging and trying to outfox the other for the sake of a measly point, Joe had a miniscule 67-point lead!

Well, who cares who wins? I thought we had decided no one would win. But no, Charlie was interested, and, I guess I am too, else I wouldn't have added up all the scores. Oh, admit it Joseph Jones, you care, of course you care, you've always cared. You care now, seeing your hard-fought lead down to a crummy 67 points. Should I tell Charlie? He'll ask me, so I have no choice. But how could he overcome so much of my lead in such a short time? He wouldn't cheat me, would he? No, but maybe, but no, goddammit, this isn't what I want out of our games. I *don't* want there to be a winner.

He forced his mind to calm down, to turn his thoughts to the spring scene outside his library window. Slowly he let his thoughts come back to the game. Yet, if there is to be a winner, I'd rather it be me. If I lose I'll always wonder how I could lose my big lead. So let it be 10,000 games. We'll play it out, then that'll be it, no more score keeping. Ten more games.

"That close, eh Joe? Hard to believe, but then we always played pretty even. So you want to quit keeping score at 10,000 games? Not quit playing, I hope."

"No, Charlie," Joe said into the phone. "I want to keep playing. I just don't want to keep scores, or ledgers, or anything. I don't want them to write on my tombstone, 'He kept score of cribbage games'."

"What would you like them to write, Joe?"

"I'd rather it said, 'He enjoyed cribbage', but my name will do nicely."

"Well, how about five games at your place Friday, then five more at my place on Saturday. That will be the big championship, OK?"

"Hmmm. Listen to us, like a couple of kids. Well, Okay, five and five this weekend."

"What about the stakes?" asked Charlie.

"Steaks! Great way to celebrate. I'll bring some, you grill 'em."

"Joe! I meant what's at stake; the prize."

"I know what you meant. Loser fixes the steaks on Sunday afternoon."

"Twenty-five years ago you said a dime a point. Since then I think we raised it to a dollar a point."

"Sure, but it's so close now that I don't think either one of us would win much anyway, but if you want, okay, a dollar a point."

"And we'll do the steaks, too, okay? Sunday afternoon, loser buys, grills, provides the beer. And we'll invite a few others over, too."

"Ok, Charlie, that way, we'll both be winners."

Joe used to be very competitive. Now he realized he had second thoughts, because more than winning, he didn't want to lose. Not winning at 10,000 games or any other number of games is fine, but I'd hate to be the loser at any point that we stop counting. So, Charlie wants to play it out, and I'm afraid he'll be upset if he loses. But it's not in me to throw the games, either. God, this is silly.

The first game, Friday night at Joe's house, actually the 9,991st game in the series, was not too dramatic. Joe gained an early lead and held it all the way to win by 19 points. The 44 points he gained for that win gave him a 111-point lead.

"A couple wins will get me back in the hunt," Charlie said as Joe dealt out the cards for the next game.

"Ah, yes, and a good start it is," he said as he surveyed the six cards he'd received.

Charlie held a wonderful hand of two 5s and two Jacks; put an 8 and a 4 in the crib for Joe, and involuntarily raised his eyebrows as he cut a Jack for the starter. Already he held twenty points, a great start at a comeback. He led a Jack, Joe countered with an 8. Charlie played his other Jack for a count of "28" and Joe played a 3 for "31" and two points.

"And the early lead," announced Joe.

Charlie now had to lead one of his 5s, Joe played a 9 for a '14' count, the last 5 was for '19', and Joe played his final card, a 6, for a '25' count and a point for the last card played.

"Well, you pegged three points, Joe, but I'm holding twenty," said Charlie as he scored his points on the pegboard.

"I've only got four. I hoped you'd cut a 7, but no such luck. Let's see what you put in my crib to go with the pair of Kings I put in. Hmmm. Great, that'll give me two points for my pair, and no help at all from you." So Charlie had an early eleven-point lead; increased it as the game progressed and for a while it looked like he might skunk Joe. But Joe hit a big 24-point hand to cut Charlie's margin of victory to only eight points.

The games went slowly as each player carefully considered his options, each point eagerly claimed, and each failure to fill a double-run groaned and lamented. They alternated winning and the five games were completed with Joe ahead by 118 points. Joe was relieved to have survived the contest so far and with his slight lead enhanced by a few points. I could probably lose three of the last five games and still win, he thought.

"I guess you'll thank me for these games, Joe. It was a good night for you."

"Are you sure you wouldn't rather play the last five now, tonight?"

"No, no. We agreed to five here and five at my place. I need the home court advantage to overcome 118 points. Now admit it, Joe, doesn't this put a little excitement into the games?"

"Quite honestly, no. It was exciting enough before, when we kept score for the evening but never bothered to accumulate the points to see who was leading. But this puts pressure into a situation that, well, I just feel like we're competing for something that doesn't exist."

"What do you mean, Joe?"

"This championship, or whatever it is; maybe it would have been better to have played a series of games, stopped, and whoever was ahead would win a dinner, then start all over with another series. But this way we're taking our entire lifetime of games and running it down to possibly one final game, winner take all."

The two grayed men sat at the kitchen table in Joe's home. They played there because they were close to the coffee and because the table was comfortable for laying out the cribbage board and the cards. A 'coffee and cribbage fest' had been their unofficial title for these events.

"But take all of what?" Joe continued. "When this is over, and one of us has won, then what? We'll look at each other and what'll we say? The loser will remember 10,000 games and think of the times he made a mistake, maybe ten, fifteen years ago that cost him a couple of points, and because of that he now 'loses' the championship of, of two old men". His arms waved through the air, as if trying to pin down a point he was trying to make.

"Yeah, you're probably right, Joe. So we'll start another 10,000 game series!"

"Ha! We should live so long!"

"If nothing else," Charlie said, "we may have the longest continuous card game in history. We should enter it in the Guinness Book of Records. I'm serious, Joe. Hey, we're friends, aren't we? We play a few games, one of us wins, one of us loses, and we go on to some more games. Maybe we'll do like you said, play a short series, then start over."

Charlie lowered his voice, said gently, "Joe, if you win, if you're ahead after the next five games I won't be upset. As you say, neither of us is really a winner or a loser. What makes 10,000 games special? If we play to 10,001 games the other guy might be ahead. But we have kept score, and it needs a finish, it needs to be completed. You wouldn't want the World Series to go on indefinitely, would you?"

Joe nodded slowly, trying to convince himself that he didn't care if he wasn't the points leader after 10,000 games. And he didn't, really, because it is just a stopping place. But gnawing at him was the question of how Charlie had managed to win so much lately, especially when the games were at his house, with his cards. If he beats me by cheating somehow, a marked deck, then what I'll have lost will be the good memories that I have of our games, of our friendship. That I couldn't forget. That's why I need to win, so I won't have to ponder that question any more.

They ate dinner together Saturday night. Charlie complained that he had been tired all day, Joe teased him that it was probably because he was up all night worrying about the last five games. Charlie replied that no, actually he'd slept well, but he ached, and Joe asked if he wanted to postpone the games, but Charlie said no, not on your life; this is a long-awaited climax that is to be savored, but not postponed.

The first game of the evening, #9,996 of the decades-long series, started badly for Joe, and he remarked that he should have had one more cup of coffee before they'd left the restaurant.

Charlie held several double-runs, a certain eight points anytime, doubled a couple of those with the help of the starter, and ran away with the game. Joe desperately tried to avoid the skunk, but the end came when he led a 7, Charlie played another 7 for two points, and Joe eagerly played his other 7 for six points, bringing him closer to avoiding the skunk. But Charlie victoriously slammed down yet another 7, pegged 12 points and reached his 121st point, ending the game, winning by 32 points. The 32 plus the 50 points for a skunk cut Joe's overall lead to a paltry 36 points. Charlie frowned and rubbed his right arm.

"You should be laughing, not frowning, Charlie"

"I just ache all over, " Charlie said as he pulled the cards in and started shuffling.

One of the ways Joe had often gained a few points on Charlie was in leading with a card of which he held pairs. If Charlie also held one of those cards and played it for a two-point peg, Joe would then play his matching card for six points. Lately, though, this hadn't worked; Joe vaguely remembered the dream in which his cards were transparent to Charlie.

In the next game Joe felt better as he had his way with the cards. Whether they were transparent or not, it was one of those games where the other guy put cards in the crib that always seemed to help his opponent. Joe almost returned the skunk, finally winning by 23 points. He felt some relief.

I just want to hold on, three more games, just hold on to my lead of 84 points and get this over with. I wonder what Charlie is thinking now—is he as concerned about winning as I am? He must be, after all, he insisted we do this. Of course, maybe to him it is just the fun of seeing where we are at 10,000 games. Besides, since he's behind he's got nothing to lose. We both know, I think, that I always won just a slight bit more so who would expect him to beat me? If he does, it will overcome years of frustration, years of knowing I was a little bit luckier with the cards. Sure, for him it's easy, but if I lose I'll always wonder how, how he could have gained so much on me in these last few games. How could my friend do this—do what? Am I already conceding that we're using a marked deck, and he's just toying with me? You always were suspicious and cynical, Jones.

"You gonna' pick up your cards, Joe?"

"Uh? Oh, yeah, sure."

"You start daydreaming now and I'll walk all over you. Let's go now, gimme something good in my crib."

His concentration wavering, Joe dumped a Jack-Queen into Charlie's crib, and winced when a King was cut as the starter. When Charlie picked up his crib at the end of the hand, he found a nice complement for the pair of tens he had put in; the double run gave him a ten-point crib, an unexpected bonus to start the game.

Joe recovered his composure and almost pulled out the game, but Charlie hung on for a slim five-point win, frowning all the way. Joe still held a 54 point lead and calculated that if he won the next game he'd have at least a 90-point lead and Charlie would then need a skunk in the final game to win it all. This thought gave him renewed interest in the next game and he played deliberately, considering the consequences of every card he played. Charlie kept frowning, took a couple of aspirin and gained a small lead by some astute (or lucky?) pegging.

The game ended rather suddenly. They were tied at 119 points apiece, Joe having rallied to catch Charlie. The game would end in the pegging phase so both players considered what would best help them in the play of the cards, not the count of the cards they held or the crib. Joe cut the deck, and Charlie turned up a Jack. In a card game that neophytes ridiculed as having silly rules, this Jack was good for two points for Charlie, and thus, the game.

Joe grunted and shook his head slowly. Charlie grunted and rubbed his arm. "Well, hmmm, what a finish. Joe, this is it, hey, the 10,000[th] game, Glad that it's come down to this. We should toast."

They toasted with some brandy to this remarkable series of games, to friendship, health, and many more years of cribbage.

"Let's hope it's a good game," said Joe.

"You mean, you win, hey?" teased Charlie, smiling for the first time since they'd sat down.

"Ok, Charlie, I lead by 27 points, so if I win this game, I'll be ahead after 10,000 games, just barely, and if you win by three points or more you'll be ahead."

"It'd be fitting if I win by two points; what are the odds that we could play 10,000 games and end up in an exact tie? Then you'd have to recheck your mathematics!"

"Not on your life, Charlie! Tonight when I go home I'll throw those books away!"

They began the 10,000th game. Joe was calm, confident. Charlie played slowly, tiredly. They savored this game, saying little except to count their points. Joe just wanted to stay close; he wouldn't mind losing if it was by less than three points. He mentally cursed the bad cards, cherished the good ones, forgetting for a time that both 'good' and 'bad' cards were an element of luck, the initial ingredient in every card game.

Joe didn't notice that Charlie was paling. Had he looked up at his friend he might have seen that Charlie wasn't just tired, but ill. But both men were so intent that they hardly noticed anything other than their cards. Even the brandy remained unfinished.

They quietly scored their way to a position of 102 points for Joe, 101 for Charlie. It was Joe's crib, which gave Charlie the right to count his points first, once they had played their cards and completed the pegging portion of the hand. With some luck either player could win it on this hand, but with first count, Charlie could count out before Joe got a chance to score his points.

Joe looked at his hand: a 4,5,6, Jack, Queen, King. Damn! A potentially nice hand, but two different sequences of three cards was not ideal. He decided that Charlie would probably want to keep lower cards to increase his chances to peg points, and would put higher cards in the crib. So he dumped the Queen-King into his crib, hoping that when combined with the starter and Charlie's contribution it would give him enough points to win the game.

Joe had figured correctly, for when Charlie looked at his hand of 4,6,7,8, Jack and King he figured it the same way. He needed to go for the win on this hand, for if the game went another hand, then Joe would have first count. He kept the numbered cards and wished for a starter that would give him a double run. The Jack-King went into Joe's crib.

Charlie cut the deck and Joe turned over a six of clubs. Neither man let show on their face that they were happy with the cut; both had 'hit': Joe now held a 4,5,6, and Jack of Diamonds, plus the starter 6, for a hand of 14 points, not counted yet, of course. Ignoring the crib because he knew that the 6 did not help the Jack-Queen he'd put in there, he needed to peg five points to reach 121, assuming Charlie didn't get to 121 first. He could try to stay away from pegging, but that would be determined by the first card that Charlie laid down.

Charlie calculated how to start. He held ten points with his 6,6,7,8,4. The 4 didn't help his hand, but it could be important in the pegging. He was uncertain how to play it; he needed twenty points to win, he held ten, and it was unlikely he'd peg ten. Yet, if Joe also held middle cards it might be impossible to avoid a series of runs that could lead to many points. He led the 7; it was the middle card of his run and gave him the best chance of catching Joe in a run; because he would count the points in his hand first, he didn't care about letting Joe peg, as long as Charlie pegged along.

Immediately Joe assumed the worst: Charlie held a double run of middle cards. He could be holding anywhere from 10 to 17 points, but he still needs to peg a few. The Jack would be the safest response, Joe thought, but would reduce his chances of pegging the five points he wanted. Of course he could forget that and hope Charlie doesn't have enough to win this hand. Except that Joe would have to lead off the next hand, and if Charlie was sitting on 119 points, he could easily peg out before Joe had a chance to score a point. Forget the next hand! Play this one, Joe!

He would keep the Jack as a safety valve; it could stop a run if needed. So he played the 6, announced the total of the two cards played, '13'. Charlie did not hesitate, for he needed points. He played the 8, announced the new total,

'21', and then, "and three points for the run". He moved his peg up three holes, to sit in the 104-point slot.

Fine, Joe said to himself, and played his 5 for '26', and four points for the run. Too late he realized his mistake; you idiot! You could have played the Jack for '31', two points, and stopped the run. Horrified he watched Charlie now play the predictable 4, for a five-card run; "Thirty, five points for the run". And a "Go", whispered Joe.

It didn't take a mathematical genius to see the situation. Joe knew it now—if Charlie's last card is a seven or an eight that will give him a hand of 12 points, and a total of 122 points when he counts. I will play the last card, for at least one point, and with my hand I'll have at least 121, except that I won't get to count. What was I thinking of? I made a rookie's error. I kept the Jack as a safety valve, and then I forget to play it, foolishly going for the four-point run. I could have settled for two points and probably made that up in the crib. But it doesn't matter now. I just have to play this card and then I'll see Charlie's 7 or 8, if that's what it is.

"I think you've got me, Charlie," Joe said, as he put down his 4.

No card was played and Joe looked up. Briefly, for less than a breath, Charlie looked at Joe, started to rub his arm ever so slowly, took a deep breath, and lowered his head to the table. The card he held fell face down onto the floor.

"Charlie! Charlie!" Joe picked up Charlie's head, felt for a pulse, in a panic tried to remember what to do in such a situation. But it didn't matter; nothing he could have done would have made any difference, the paramedics told him later.

"It was probably quite painless, and quick."

Joe came back to Charlie's later that night. The door was unlocked and he let himself into the quiet house. In the living room on the table lay the cards, the pegboard, two empty coffee cups, and two brandy snifters, each with a small amount of golden-brown liquid in them. Joe picked up the deck, then let the cards slip out of his hand, to drop softly onto the table, as noiselessly as butterflies landing on a flower. He looked at the pile near where he'd been sitting a couple of hours earlier. There lay the 6,5, and 4 he had played. He turned over what he knew was his Jack. Then he turned over the four cards that constituted his crib. He saw the Jack, Queen, and two Kings and laughed at himself. I had it easily; should have played the Jack. Lastly he looked at the other cards, Charlie's cards. He saw the 7, the 8, and the 4. On the floor was the last card, the all-mighty card that would put a cap on 10,000 games, making one of them the winner. He picked it up and laid it on the table, still face down.

Who wins, Charlie or me? Does it matter? Does Charlie know? Did he die knowing he won? Did he, God forbid, use a marked deck? No, I'll assume he did not, especially since he might be able to read my thoughts now. No, neither of us won, and we both won. We won because we enjoyed a close friendship that survived conflicts much more important than a game of cards. And I don't want to know. Yes, I'll feel bad if the card is a 7 or an 8; how strange—if this card is a lousy 7 or 8, I'll feel bad. Don't I feel bad enough with Charlie gone? This is dumb. Forgive me Charlie, for wondering if you went too far in wanting to win; I don't believe it.

Joe took Charlie's fourth card and stuck it in the deck of cards, then picked up the other cards, shuffled them all together and threw them in the trash.

This is not so much a story as a collection of memories about the dogs that Gaye and I have had together. If you're reading this you've probably heard these stories, so you may want to skip this syrupy piece.--erw

Do Dogs Dream?

One thing I've noticed about dogs is that they seem to adjust more quickly and easily to traumatic changes in their lives.

For example, one night Bret, one of the Cocker Spaniels that have graced our lives, woke up in the middle of the night, and his moving around woke me, too. Bret had already had eye problems and had had surgery on one eye to relieve the pain, and could now see only out of the other one. He seemed distressed and confused and I realized that he seemed unable to see at all.

There wasn't anything to do about it at 3 A.M. in the morning except cuddle him, but first thing in the morning I took him to the vet. Yes, he was indeed blind; it had just happened. Of course, as we already knew, he'd had numerous vision problems that had resulted in the surgery and loss of the one eye. Now, (thankfully with no apparent pain), the other eye had just shut down.

All of his life I'd noticed that Bret did not like it when I threw a ball, or anything else, up in the air for him to catch. He seemed to lose sight of it. He acted afraid that he was going to be hit by the object. Now, I realized that he'd always had a problem with his vision; he may have only had tunnel vision and no peripheral vision at all, his entire life.

But as I was getting to, he adjusted quickly. Of all the dogs I've had, and they all show levels of intelligence if you are willing to teach them things, Bret was the smartest and easiest to train. He learned things so fast I wondered where he got his vocabulary. He could be out in the park running wildly after squirrels, but if I whistled he would stop and look back at me waiting for a follow-up command. Sometimes I just said, "Wait for me, Bret", and he would stand there and wait. Other times I would say, "Come on back," and he would, reluctantly, give up the chase and return promptly. No big deal? Remember, I said promptly; most dogs have to be told several times before they'll obey, or else they'll return only with numerous stops to smell and mark on the way. He just seemed to know what I wanted and I never had to spend much time training him.

When I would walk Bret and Bart in the mountains Bret was the adventurous one; he would run ahead to see what was around the next bend. Bart always stayed close by. But Bret paid attention to where we were. Usually before I could call to him Bret would come running back as if to see if we were still coming. If I wanted to start back, I just said so; if we were to continue, I would say, "It's okay, Bret, go on," and he would dash off again.

Bret was the best hunter of all our dogs, and Bart did pretty well too. Between the two of them they caught several birds, some in the yard and others while hiking with me. Bret also stalked lizards in the backyard. He would stand perfectly still for several minutes, pointing (where did he learn that?) at a lizard sunning itself on the block wall. He caught more than I can remember. Once he walked into the house and fortunately met me before Gaye. He had a long one hanging out of his mouth, tail sticking out one side, the head out the other. Poor thing must have been in shock. I said, "Bret, you better get out here with that thing before you're Mom sees it". He obediently turned around and took his prize outside. Another time I wasn't home to intervene and he did bring Gaye a gift. Walked into Gaye's office and put it on the floor by the side of her desk. Gaye looked down to see a dead bird. Good boy, Bret

So anyway now he can't see; how will he join us on walks? He and Bart I could take with no leash because they obeyed so well and didn't do stupid things like try to catch cars. But when we walked for a long ways or where there were busy streets I usually leashed them.

The first day out after he lost his vision I began to teach him, "Step down" (at the curb), and "Step up", at the other side of the street. Again, he learned this so well and so fast it amazed me. To watch him trot along smelling his way it was hard to believe he couldn't see. I'm sure he missed 'seeing' the cats and squirrels and other dogs along our regular route, but his nose kept him busy and seemingly happy.

As I write this there is another Cocker Spaniel, Tracy, lying in the hallway, napping. He is always nearby, never letting me get too far away. If he wakes from a nap the first thing he does he check where I'm at. Occasionally he whimpers, almost a bark, and his breathing will speed up. Is he dreaming? Of what? Sounds like he may be chasing the squirrel that runs along the wires that cross our yard! Or maybe he's dreaming of a game of 'yellow ball'. Of all our Cocker Spaniels none have loved to play ball as much as Tracy. And none have latched on to a favorite toy the way he has to his yellow ball. Not that he understands the coloring, but he has learned which ball I mean when I say, "get your yellow ball".

Usually I haven't had to tell him to find it, because for years he would come running with it in his mouth when I came home from work. I could barely change clothes he was so eager to go out to the backyard where we could play with the yellow ball. When he was younger he'd go forever; I'd have to call off the game. Now, as he nears nine years old, the games are very short. But he still keeps track of the ball. It has become a joke around here to note where the yellow ball shows up. Tracy will pick it up and move it around, sometimes to the outside, but usually into the house. Sometimes I see it and wonder, how many of these yellow balls are there?

Speaking of adjusting to changes, he and I have both adjusted well to my retirement. He still has that inner clock in him that stirs him around five o'clock. He comes to me and in his dog's way tells me its time to go out into the back yard, even if we don't play with any of his several balls. There are still odors to smell, plants to mark, birds to chase away, and people to watch as they pass by the path in the field behind our house. Of course, he assumes I am just as interested in these things as he is.

So dogs play, maybe they dream, they can learn, they love to smell every blade of grass and every plant and every piece of garbage they can find in the street, but can they think?

Sometimes I think that if dogs had a voice box and thumbs they would be a challenge to Homo sapiens for control of the planet.

If a dog shares with his friend, did he think that out? You could call it instinct, because it is certainly instinctive for an adult wolf to share its food with the pups. But is it instinctive to share soiled tissues?

One evening Gaye and I and some friends were sitting around our family room, talking about this and that. I had allergies and kept wiping my runny nose with tissues. The balled up tissues began to pile up on the ledge next to where I was sitting. Now I don't know exactly why dogs like to chew on tissues. Maybe it's no different than people chewing on gum—it's taste good! Bret was eyeing the growing pile of tissues, which he knew he wasn't supposed to go after. He'd been told that many times after he'd stolen some out of the trash. I know, that blows my theory that he was very smart because he learned so well, but as kids, did we do everything we were told to do? No, not if it was something that was fun to do and we thought we could get away with it!

So finally Bret jumps up on my lap, as he often did in the evening. So okay, lay down. But no, he then practically climbed all over me to reach a tissue. For some reason I didn't say anything; I just watched him. He grabbed a tissue in his mouth and climbed down. Then he went over to his brother Bart, who was lying on the floor being a good boy, and gave the tissue to Bart! He then duplicated his efforts and climbed back up to get another tissue for himself! After laughing I traded them a cookie for the tissues.

Bret and Bart got along so well we are sure they were mind melded; one mind and soul in two bodies. They did everything together. One would look at the other and suddenly they'd run outside and play 'charger'. This was a game in which one would go to one end of the yard and the other would go to the opposite end. They would run at each other, crash like jousting knights, then run back and do it again. I swear, I saw them do this may times. Or, they'd get that look and run outside and do, well, do their business.

Spencer and Tracy didn't get along as well, though they too played together. They just needed to vie for attention when I got home from work, not like Bret and Bart who shared my pats and displayed nary a bit of jealousy.

Spencer was a tough little guy and when I got home he wanted me to pay attention to him, and him alone. Tracy wanted the same thing and Spencer, who was much stronger, belted poor Tracy around a few times.

They were all handsome dogs (Tracy still is). Maybe because they came first, our finest dog memories will probably always be of Bret and Bart: of walks in the neighborhood, Bret in the snow at Mammoth, Bart smelling the flowers in the neighborhood, (or of digging out of the yard then getting stuck in the neighbor's yard, and crying pitifully at their gate, while Bret, who was able to squeeze out of the neighbor's yard, shivered at our front door waiting for us to come home)!

Or of cleaning stickers out of their fur after I had hiked with them. I learned, though, so Spencer and Tracy haven't had the fortune to hike in the mountains with me; too hard to clean them up.

Or of them running, running, running in the park, with ears flopping as they chased the wind, or me, or a flock of crows that had dared to land in their park. Or of Bart walking around the house squeaking his toy hamburger. (Bart liked food, even in his toys.)

Okay, enough. Just one more thing: Bret and Bart were a couple of hams. Really, they loved to have their picture taken and I just had to bring out the camera and they would pose. For those of you who haven't seen my favorite picture of them, just ask sometimes; I bet you'll swear it was professionally posed and taken. But it was just them hamming it up for me and I took it with one shot, no playing around trying to set it up.

Spencer, the puppy who had such a short life, left his memories too. He was our champion digger. It was like in the cartoons where the animated dog is digging furiously with dirt flying out of the growing hole and piling up in back of him. Looking for... a bone? A mole? China? Spencer lived with us for one summer, so often his digging was to find a cool spot in which to take a break. He was good at digging up plants, too. One day Gaye was in the back yard planting flowers, once again trying to get some color in the yard that would survive the trampling of puppies. I happen to look up from whatever chore I was engaged in and had to just stand back and watch the scene for a while. Finally I said to Gaye, "Do you see what your dogs are doing?" Trailing behind her, Spencer and Tracy were mimicking Gaye's work by digging up the plants after she had stuck them in the ground!

To try to restrain Spencer and Tracy from totally destroying the plants, I put up a screen all along the edge of the yard where the lawn met the planted area. This worked for awhile, my hope being that by the time they got big enough to leap over the screen they would be calmer. Then one day they realized they were big enough to do just that; at the southern end of the yard the screen had slipped down just enough so that they could jump over it. One would run the length of the yard and leap over and the other would follow, looking like the sheep that an insomniac counts. So I took the screen down, a futile project abandoned. Then I saw Spencer and Tracy race across the yard and when they came to the spot where they had been leaping, they did so again, even though the screen was no longer there! They repeated this several times before it dawned on them that they did not have to jump anymore. But don't people get into habits sometimes that can be just as silly?

Speaking of silly, I once heard an interpretation of what heaven might be like. That it will be filled with the wonders that we individually enjoy. Some things we may all enjoy, but it'd be a little different for everybody. So, would it be too crazy to expect there to be healthy dogs running around with their ears flapping, or digging holes that go nowhere but are fun to dig, or walking around the neighborhood smelling for other dogs, cats and just good, smelly things? And what would heaven be to a dog? Does a dog dream of a heaven where he is with 'his people?' Or does he dream of being with other dogs, cats, and birds?

www.ingramcontent.com/pod-product-compliance
Lightning Source LLC
Chambersburg PA
CBHW050947120626
46552CB00001B/418